MW01241710

Stories *OFF* the Garden Path

stories by

Carl F. Thompson, Jr.

MAIN STREET RAG PUBLISHING COMPANY
CHARLOTTE, NORTH CAROLINA

ACKNOWLEDGEMENTS

descant: "Orals"
Everything But the Baby: "The Social Compact"
The Main Street Rag: "Para-Pet"
Phantasmagoria: "The Ladies in Waiting"
The William and Mary Review: "Anna's Head"
Thin Air: "Mrs. Harris Admires the Perseids"

Library of Congress Control Number: 2011935280

ISBN: 978-1-59948-308-5

Produced in the United States of America

Main Street Rag
PO Box 690100
Charlotte, NC 28227
www.MainStreetRag.com

To Patricia, who's wise enough never to trust my driving

CONTENTS

ORALS

I tell my dark and glossy-haired dental hygienist Erin—
she who diverts attention even garbed in blue surgical
mask and scrubs—what I always tell her: that I long for
nothing less than the final achievement of wholly painless
dentistry. Not that I can say so while she's got one of her
dental picks scraping away as if she were doing a dig at a
Mayan archaeological site. Who can say anything once the
hygienist (worse, the dentist) has one of those instruments
exorcising the evil spirits—plaque, gingivitis, who knows
what all—from your teeth and gums?

"No, I mean it," I say, when I'm finally allowed to press
the little button that runs water into the blue Dixie cup I
then proceed to flush my mouth from.

"And I totally agree," responds Erin.

As I'm sure she does. As it so happens, every time I switch
dentists, I seem to have a thing with my dental hygienist. I
dated Christine for a year, but that was a dentist ago. Then
I moved to Baltimore. Erin is tall—she may have an inch
on me—but she is amply ample where amplitude should
be and precisely, unambiguously scalloped where scallops
should be; I can tell, scrubs or not. She exceeds comely. She
has one of those come-hither-thou, launch-a-few-hundred-

ships, lets-start-a-war kind of faces. Plus (sans mask) her gleaming-white teeth. If only she weren't engaged to a fellow who lives a hundred miles away she sees weekends. What business has a thirty-year-old female got these days, chaining herself to someone pre-wedlock? (An unbiased thirty-two-year-old male asks.) Is it even fashionable? It's a crime, but okay, okay, I observe the presumed chivalric code nonetheless.

So, she's got perfect teeth, something that cannot be said for me, not with my incisors nor my bicuspids nor my molars, upper or lower. I'm the patient of patients, the true $$ dollar sign walk-in gift to any dentist, honest or no. Not that I classify Dr. Dameroth as among the sort that takes advantage. Ten teeth crowned so far, but that's only because I'm counting.

"So," I say, continuing on, "my theme of totally pain-free dentistry. There could be any number of solutions. If desired, an iPod—or better, a small DVD player visible despite the dentist's head movements or the brightness of the overhead lights. It may require a set of mirrors to pass the image from one place to another to avoid visual obstructions. Or maybe it could be one of those systems that projects an image onto eyeglasses. Not sure how those work. What else? A massage and a pedicure. If a manicure could be worked out without interfering with the dental work, that gets added. Maybe it gets worked in between times, when the dentist temporarily steps away from the patient. Several possibilities there."

"Who gives the massage? How does a masseuse or masseur or whoever work without interfering with the dentist? And do you mean one of those fish pedicures?" Erin is already laughing at the impracticality of my suggestions, but she's all for playing this game out.

"Fish pedicures?"

"Yeah. Where you put your feet in a bowl of water with fish that eat off any excess, scaly skin you may have. Tidies things up."

"You're kidding." (*Is* she kidding?) "No, we use a massage chair. All the dental chairs get retrofitted for inbuilt massage units that work like regular massage chairs."

"But all that machinery rolling up and down the patient's back means his mouth will never be stable. It'll move in and out as the rollers stroll back-and-forth over the patient's back. The dentist would be constantly chasing the tooth with his drill. It'd be like walking a tightrope built with the elasticity of a trampoline."

"Boy, are you negative."

"Hold still a minute," she says, scraping one of my teeth with a little more rigor than I favor. She scrapes for a gratingly long time, one or two minutes solid, before I emerge for a gasp of water from that dinky blue cup.

"Employ on-staff massage therapists," I say. "Or train the dental technicians. There's always some time that the dentist has to mosey off and leave the patient by himself, either to attend a second patient, or look at someone the hygienist has just examined, or examine X-rays, or reshape some dental fixture—the edge of a crown, for example. Or that period when the dentist walks off after administering Novocaine, waiting for the anesthetic to penetrate—better yet—saturate. During that whole time—"

But she's in my mouth again. "So you're saying a massage therapist stands by for action during idle times—for example, that seven minutes when the patient must keep his mouth absolutely clamped down on that putty-like stuff we use to take dental impressions, right?"

"R-a-a-a-h ..." I can't even say "right."

"Cute idea. Not sure I've heard that one before. But it'd cost too much. Have you seen what a massage therapist charges? We'd almost certainly have to pay a full day's labor, even though the work would be part-time."

"N-a-a-h-t ..." Not ...

"I hear you, Cuthbert."

"P-u-h-l ..." Please.

"Cuth. Here's a secret: Don't speak when you can't. Why don't you spit that out?"

The cup emptied, I settle back into the chair, actually wriggling about, hunting for true comfort, so that as Erin leans over again, she's pressing her body against mine to contest my wriggling. I don't know when we started playing this game. Two years ago by now?

"And a totally new concept for the waiting room," I note. "TVs, DVDs, the Internet, all accessible, nothing played over loudspeakers general ... guh ... ly."

"Better chairs and cushions, too," Erin adds.

"Ahh ..rt ..wok ..."

"Artwork, yes, but that's so subjective, Cuth. Don't you like Dr. Dameroth's paintings? He does his own artwork, you know."

"F-f-ine for a dent—"

"Fine for a dentist. That's judgmental, you know."

She's now down to flossing. Every tooth, every cranny, every crevice, every back alleyway, she masters. I've frequently admitted I can't reach more than half the places she can—a physical impossibility.

"So, how's your love life?" I finally chuck in. My off-the-cuff camouflage question, as if I'm only concerned for her. But I also like jangling her nerves. I like stretching any pause I can muster rather than dueling in my mouth, even a change in dental floss.

"I'm still closer to my dog than my man," she says.

"Are you saying your man is a dog?"

She stretches far across my body and centers her eyes on mine. "No, Cuth, would that I could be so merciless."

"Then be ruthless, *be* merciless—indeed diabolical ..."

"This from the man who's trying to redesign our dental office for charm and perfectly pain-free dental care?"

"Let us not in all things consistent be."

"Oh, boy, that's one I won't quote."

Her head's nearly in my mouth, zipping up and down the aisles between my teeth with the floss.

"Has anyone every talked to you about the River Floss…" I venture.

"The George Eliot novel? Yes, those liking to delay some aspect of the hygiene process. Cuth, do you really find all this so uncomfortable?"

Of course I now unexpectedly swallow some saliva and more or less spasm and gasp momentarily—after which Erin plunges right in again.

I start inventorying the subjects I could bring up that would prolong the visit, keep her face and that very supple body closely pressed. The upcoming summer? Vacation plans? Her mother's health? Is she still skeet-shooting? She mentioned that her fiancé liked to shoot ducks and they'd gone skeet-shooting once. When she bends her head to study something in my lower jaw, I see her midnight black hair, so exquisitely parted down the precise middle of her head, like a signature of the meaning of her life—a good person, a direct path. That's different from me, even though my path in life looks similar. My affection for the direct path is to too-timidly hove to the narrow. I should take up a machete and hack my way into the rainforest. As Andrew Marvell said to his coy mistress, we only have so many rainforests to play in during our lives, who says we may in any gardens frolic to-and-fro afterwards?

She's daubing her toothbrush, reminding me somehow of Van Gogh dabbling with a palette in the field. Black birds fly overhead in mysterious Vs—Van Gogh's bird-wings. We're nearing the end.

"So what—besides yourself—is your boyfriend's favorite toy?"

"A Harley, Cuth, and don't refer to me as anybody's toy."

"Wasn't serious. I just meant … what flavor is thish—?"

"Peach," she says, delving to the back molars first.

I hate peach-flavored toothpaste. I want to ask her when her boyfriend is finally going to make up his mind. They've been engaged or semi-engaged the three years I've been coming to Dr. Dameroth's. I'm not sure she's satisfied with the relationship—she's thrown out too many barbs lately and on good days we bandy jokes back and forth like shuttlecocks, so much so that her attentiveness to my mouth is such that my teeth leave in pretty much the condition as when I arrived. Hygienic industry overcome by flirtation. But then, I did mention chivalry, didn't I?

Too soon, she drops her dental mask and presses the buzzer to summon Dr. Dameroth. She's ready for him to give me the once-over.

"So what else can we use to improve dental relations?" I toss into the slowly moving river of speech.

"Hmm. Dental 'relations,'" she responds. "That does take work."

"The pain-free dental office is still miles in the future?"

"Not light years. But I think you stepped a little aside with that last question."

"Well, how much of an interest do you have in this concept as … a project?"

"One that would undo my vast experience with skeet-shooting and motorcycles? So far, I don't think you've laid out a practical-sounding program. Maybe dentistry for California, but for Baltimore …?"

"Okay," I say, trying to think freely. "Overhead mobiles for children."

"Dr. Dameroth doesn't take patients under age twelve."

"Overhead mobiles for the very old. Alzheimer's patients. Might amuse them."

"Well, with Alzheimer's, you can never predict. They might ignore the mobiles—never even notice them, or they might be obsessed, springing out of the chair to knock them about."

"Language lessons. As an iPod option to music."

"Sessions are too short to usefully learn language. And usually patients only come two or three times a year."

"You really did learn skeet-shooting, didn't you?"

"I'm used to shooting at … cow patties." She smiles and gives me a left-hand jab to the upper right arm. "Come on," she says, "you can do better than this. Give me three good ones."

"And?"

"And. First, get 'em."

"Cotton cigarettes for ex-smokers—or current smokers— to suck on, like when we were kids. Or liquor-flavored lollipops."

"Nope. Liquor license."

"Really? Bigger bibs. Sometimes I dribble on my tie."

Erin makes a wavy, "iffy" motion with the flat of her hand. "Sometimes you dribble on your tie because of all the Novocaine you ask for. It'd be a change from standard. We'd have to look at costs and availability and patient likes and dislikes."

"A brainstorming group to meet after hours to examine optimum treatment comforts."

"Anyone can form a committee. A committee's not an idea. Come on, I'm worth three good ideas, right?"

"What is it—do you just think that people should suffer?"

"Some people, sure." Is she laughing at one such person?

Dr. Dameroth steps in.

"Just three and out, huh?" I say, as Erin steps out of the hygienist's room.

"Three what?" Dr. Dameroth inquires.

"I don't know," I say. "Lost my train of thought."

"And you're …" he reaches to check my chart.

"Thirty-two," I say, not thinking.

"Great age," he responds. Dr. Dameroth is in his mid-fifties. "Shoot women out of the trees like they were birds."

"Watch it, Doc," I caution with mirth, "that sounds like a line from *Alfie*." That's the Michael Caine movie remade decades later with Jude Law. Alfie the hero is a demonstrably self-centered being who constantly refers to women as "birds."

"If you try to PC me, I'll just find another tooth to crown."

"What are we up to now, per, doctor?"

"Oh, I think, but don't quote me, one thousand seventy-one dollars. Wait till next year."

Afterwards, I'm standing just outside Erin's office, by the office computer. "How much?" I ask Erin.

"One hundred nineteen dollars today. No X-rays. A gift. We need to set your next appointment." She names a date six months off. I say "Why not?" She scribbles on the appointment card.

She starts to duck back into the hygienist's room, when I tap a finger to her left shoulder.

"What if I keep working on my ideas during the meantime. I could actually call and leave them with the receptionist."

"Who's me, half the time."

"Well, I could just call you, then. You're still living alone?"

"What's in it for me?"

"Dinner?"

She crosses her arms and looks at me soberly. She has extraordinarily dark, attentive eyes.

I downshift. "Lunch?"

"We never eat lunch here. He works us to death."

"Yeah, but aren't you off—doesn't the office close—Thursdays?"

"You don't know where I live. It might be miles and miles."

"You said your mother lives in Dundalk. How many miles is that?"

"It's gotta be now," she says.

"You mean, eat now? Let's go."

"No, I mean, play your silly game *now*. You've gotta have absolute winners."

"One, fish tanks and colorful birds in each room."

"Upkeep!" She counters.

"Two, air fresheners everywhere."

"Isn't that just cosmetic? Is it a real comfort? What if someone's allergic?"

"A ten-percent reduction for patients who pay in cash."

"Oh, hell," she says. "That might actually be good. Takes analysis."

"Well, that still can't exhaust everything. Give me another chance. Let me call you."

"What's the matter, Cuth, you've had three years to do that." She smiles maliciously, raises her dental mask like an armored faceplate, and calls for someone named Malcolm Healy in the waiting room.

"But you're engaged."

"Yeah. *Have been for six years*."

But now she's waving bye-bye as she shakes hands with Mr. Healy, a half-decent looking fellow somewhere in his mid-thirties, who, if he's not chivalrous, might steal out of midair the information I've just pried loose.

Me? I've lost. I exit the office, fiddle with the appointment card, trying to tuck it into my wallet when I bump into a woman and drop the card.

"Sorry," I say, another gorgeous thing walking into Dameroth's office. How does he do that, anyway?

Picking up the card from the carpet, I notice a ten-digit set of numbers scribbled on the backside.

"Huh." I can't help but say it out loud.

GARY'S SEAT

Jim and Carol hadn't driven into town to see the national Christmas tree since Gary had been eight. They might have had things been otherwise, but of course things never are otherwise.

They still lived in their comfortable Dutch colonial surrounded by tall oaks, now edged by snow. Jim ran his dental practice from home in the addition they'd built when they bought the house fourteen years ago. Each would turn forty next year. They were well off, in the prime of their lives.

As always, Christmas Eve, when it arrived, signaled well-established traditions: hot cocoa, cookies, and Christmas music played against a background of firelight and the lights of the Christmas tree. By five p.m., dusk had turned to nightfall. While Carol worked at cookies and cocoa, Jim gathered himself from his chair to head to the woodpile. But as he stood—for the barest instant—he thought he'd glimpsed Gary in the wingchair opposite. Not likely. Not in that stiff chair, though it held the best view of the tree. Or did Gary's tastes and tolerances change with age?

Daydreaming—Gary's fondest game had been "pretend"—wasn't helping Jim get firewood. He fetched a coat and work gloves and under the floodlights traipsed out the back onto a hard and crunchy three-inch layer of snow.

He knew it was too early yet for Gary. He probably hadn't seen a thing at all, nothing but a sliver of imagination, his habit of letting anticipation get the better of him.

Pulling back the tarp from the woodpile, he collected five fair-sized logs in his canvas carrier, and added twigs for kindling.

"Now, that I like," said Carol when the fire took hold. "What could be better than Christmas Eve other than Christmas itself?"

And they glared into the fire and shuddered as if the room had turned cold.

On Christmas morning, the phone rang as soon as Jim and Carol had finished their breakfast of glazed cinnamon rolls. Each hesitated, looking from one to the other. Finally, Carol took it, smiling only mildly warily. "Hello? Uncle Walter! Well, merry Christmas to you, *too*." Jim, trying to be nonchalant, barely raised his eyebrows. "Oh, we're *so* sorry to hear that." She made a face at Jim, something between disappointment and the expected what-can-you-do. They'd had a somewhat bad track record the last two years. Jim could see it was about to be three. "No, no, don't worry about *that*, Uncle Walter. It'd be absolutely irrational to think such a thing. Well, we certainly hope Lucille improves."

Hanging up, she said, "They can't make it. Lucille has bronchitis."

"My side of the family again," said Jim. "If it's bronchitis, you'd think he could have called yesterday or even earlier. You don't get that overnight, or do you?"

"Well, there's still Frank and Edna and Melinda. Though it would have been nicer with Walter and Lucille. That great big dinner table and all that empty space. At least we've never had a Christmas where everyone bowed out." She managed a fragile, somewhat posed, smile. "And there's no reason to think …"

"Absolutely," her husband soundly affirmed. "No reason at all."

Dinner was set for two-thirty. Frank and Edna arrived at one. Their daughter Melinda, a twenty-six year-old school teacher in Baltimore, followed them by a half hour. Edna was some sixteen years older than her sister Carol. In the last few years, a thyroid problem had turned Edna slightly bug-eyed. It was a look people grew used to. But Melinda, in Jim's judgment, was a walking case of anorexia—as thin as beef jerky—with a scrawny enough personality to match. As always, she wore an impenetrable black outfit, so close-fitting it seemed shrink-wrapped.

"Walter can't make it?" Frank, a large but pleasant sixty-year-old with a bulbous nose, looked wary. He was halfway into his first Bud. "How can that be?"

Jim was adding a log to the fire.

"Yeah, he can't make it."

"Oh, how *terrible*!" said Edna. She looked appalled.

"Now, it doesn't mean a thing," cautioned Jim.

"How *can* you think it's terrible, Edna?" Carol said, holding a corkscrew and an unopened bottle of Chardonnay. Edna was standing next to Frank in the kitchen doorway. "You can't say such things."

"Right. It's just unfortunate, nothing more," agreed Frank, briefly putting an arm around his wife's shoulders.

A small swirl of anxious but gallant smiles circled among the party members, all but Melinda, who seemed fascinated by a small spider web she'd found in the gap between a corner of the living room ceiling and the top of a bookcase.

"Here, let me help you with that," Frank said to Carol, taking the bottle and working the corkscrew. "Who wants?" he said, holding the opened bottle aloft. "Edna?"

"Yes, I'll have some."

Carol said, "The glasses are right in there, Frank."

"After these last few Christmases, I'm already trained," Frank said, proceeding to the cabinet.

Melinda helpfully reported, "Just show me to the vermouth, the essentials, and a martini glass. Olives?"

"In that little shelf beside the salad dressings. Toothpicks right there in the mug by the countertop TV. Gin, vodka, down there."

Standing near the dining room table, Jim queried Frank on what retirement finally felt like. "Like plunging into an ocean. Edna's lined up a dozen cruise options. It's the Caribbean or the Med, I guess. Here I am sixty, retired a month, and I guess I'm going to end up among all those blue-haired ladies on one of those liners where everyone looses their money at the slots between ports or gets some ghastly intestinal thing."

Jim clapped a hand on his brother-in-law's shoulder. "Well, we're glad to see you could make it for Christmas, again. Family means so much to us."

"Our third year in a row and though we'd never think of standing you up, you really should allow us to reciprocate sometime."

"But then what would we do with this big table?"

To which Frank offered no response.

Carol was still prepping in the kitchen, so people continued talking and drinking. Melinda, in particular, as she thought the Stoli grand.

Their rosewood dining table—covered with a red-and-green plaid Christmas tablecloth—was large. It seated eight without extensions, a dozen with. Jim had the extensions in, as if preparing for a dozen. Each side now seated five, instead of three, plus the two end chairs. The table had been new two Christmases ago. While of course it mattered to Jim and Carol that they'd only had Gary, they considered their extended family just that—family and everything that family represented: closeness, bonhomie, the pleasing presence of human goodwill.

In a goodwill spirit, Jim noticed Melinda making by his count her third martini, and he noticed Frank noticing, too. Spirits, Jim thought ironically.

"So let's see, where should we sit?" Edna looked from Carol to Jim.

Jim had it all in hand: seating arrangements that would distribute five people across twelve chairs. "Edna, I thought you could sit over here, just two chairs down on the left from Carol at the end, with Melina two chairs down from you, and that would give room—ample room, admittedly," he said, jokingly, "for Frank on the starboard side middle, with Carol and I anchoring the ends." This meant, from where Jim sat at the head of the table, that Frank would be seated in the third of five chairs to Jim's right, Carol at the foot of the table, and Melinda and Edna in the second and fourth chairs to Jim's left, respectively. It looked like this:

Empty   Melinda   Empty   Edna   Empty

Jim   Carol

Empty   Empty   Frank   Empty   Empty

"You know, you're the only husband I've ever seen dictate the seating arrangements," Frank observed.

Laughing, Carol said, "I quite agree."

"If I were married, I'd let my husband do it," Melinda chimed. "If he wanted."

"Anyone in mind?" queried a dubious Edna.

"Don't look so perplexed, Momma. I'm just sleeping around."

Seeking to divert this probable (she suspected) piece of disinformation, Carol asked, "Why is it, Jim, that you always spread people out this way?"

Her husband quickly responded, "It serves the illusion of having even more company."

Edna said, "We're not enough?"

"Actually, with everyone spread out this way, isn't it like there's fewer of us, not more?" Melinda challenged.

"It's somehow-or-other Jim's new practice at Christmas," noted Carol. "New since getting this table, at any rate. You remember, last year there were seven of us, which would have fit the table's normal eight seats almost perfectly, but he still put the extensions in and spaced out five individual gaps in the seating? Five unfilled chairs?"

"Yes, now, that's right, I suppose," replied Edna.

"It is, Edna," Carol assured.

"So the extensions are *still* in," mused Frank almost cheerily, as if it were a puzzle to solve.

Carol glanced at Jim where he sat a mile away at the head of the table, before she changed track: "Anyway, I thought I'd do things a bit differently this year. The ham instead of turkey—Jim's trip to HoneyBaked yesterday—with my own raisin sauce, then the mashed potatoes, and the sweet potatoes roasted instead of the usual candied ones with marshmallows."

Privately, Jim envisioned how Gary, who even at their earlier tables, sat in the chair to Jim's left, had always liked candied sweet potatoes.

"So we had twelve chairs last year, just for the seven of us. That hadn't really sunk in on me," said Frank.

"Yes, Frank, that's right," Carol confirmed. "Though if Jim's Uncle Oliver and Aunt Gwen had made it as planned, there would have been nine."

There was an awkward hush around the table. Everyone seemed to have frozen in place, except for Melinda. Carol could have bit her tongue.

"If they were alive, would you still have invited them this year?" Melinda played with an olive, pushing it here-and-there in her glass.

Edna positively glowered at her daughter.

Not having done enough damage, Melinda plowed right on, "Well, I always thought Oliver a bit of a tightwad, didn't you?"

"Nonsense. He was a chivalrous man," said her mother, starkly embarrassed.

"He was always courteous," said Carol. She quickly asked, "Jim, do you think you'd like to give thanks about *now*?"

"Sure, right. Let's all hold hands, everyone." The party of five stood from their remotely spaced chairs and stretched to grasp fingertips. Frank, the most isolated, weaved slightly from the effort but—thanks in no small measure to his size—retained his balance.

Jim intoned a short prayer that included a blessing for their guests. "And please, Lord, bless Walter and Lucille, who were not able to join us this year, but whom we hope will be with us next year ... in body or in spirit ... Amen."

Everyone chimed in "Amen," too, and took their seats.

"'In body or in spirit'—you said that last year, too, didn't you?" remarked Melinda.

"Hmm?" replied Jim.

"When you say Grace you say, we hope those who didn't make it this year will make it next, 'in body or in spirit.'"

"Do I?"

"Anyway, Oliver was selfish," said Melinda, returning unimpeded to her earlier target. "Now if you want to think of someone as 'chivalrous'—who still uses that term anyway?—it would have been Jim's Uncle Howard. He looked rather like a knight in shining armor, I always thought. 'Sir' Uncle Howard, let's say—and wouldn't that have made Jim's Aunt Ellen, 'Lady' Ellen?"

Carol said, "Jim, would you like to start serving?"

Jim knew this was the part of Christmas dinner that he both hated and loved. First his discomfort level surged, then abated, to be overcome in the end with an undeniable sense of *radiance*.

Melinda continued, "I say that about Uncle Howard even though everyone knows Howard lied two years ago about why he and Ellen couldn't come for Christmas dinner."

"Melinda!" Edna looked beside herself.

"And I know that's what everyone thinks about Oliver and Gwen last year."

"We'll go counterclockwise," said Jim, moving the mounded bowl of mashed potatoes to his right.

"Everyone sleeps around, Mother. And regardless of whatever good qualities he may have had, Howard was a womanizer and if he hadn't been with that other woman, Ellen wouldn't have been with that other man, and they'd have both come for Christmas two years ago, and then they could have come to last year's Christmas, too, but of course by then they were dead because Ellen couldn't stand it any longer."

Meanwhile, passing the potatoes to his right, Jim watched—he could never quite figure this out, how his perceptions or hallucinations or real seeing never led to any visual disturbances by any other guests—Jim watched as his Uncle Howard, a very large man with a very large appetite, took a giant helping of mashed potatoes. Jim glared at him, but Howard merely passed the potatoes on to Frank, who took less than a giant helping, but a pretty big one nonetheless. Not that any of the guests at the table had spied the handoff, Jim knew. For reasons he could never fathom, he was the perennial privileged audience for these Christmas table antics, he and he alone. To anyone else, it looked as if he, Jim, had handed the potatoes to Frank directly. After all, Uncle Howard didn't even exist.

"So, Edna," said Carol, carefully ignoring Melinda, "your last email said you two were planning a cruise?"

Jim's Aunt Ellen, one chair removed from Frank and happily three chairs removed from Howard, was now helping herself to potatoes, too. She'd already dipped one large spoonful, then said, "It's always so darn difficult to shake mashed potatoes off the spoon, isn't it?" She studied the situation, then spooned a second dollop, using her naked finger to rake the spoon clean, eyeing Jim squarely as if saying two half spoonfuls was no more than fair. But Ellen had always been a wisp of a thing, so Jim didn't think he should hold it against her as she passed the potatoes on to Carol. Jim resolved not to look at either Ellen's or Howard's head wounds during the course of the meal, though in truth he thought they looked politely small, as fatal bullet wounds go. Not that he knew anything about forensic pathology. Not that he knew why he and only he could see these people or hear them speak.

"Yes, Carol, we've found what looks to be an excellent cruise on the Rhine."

"Oh, how nice."

"The Rhine?" said Frank. He looked perplexed. "The Rhine?"

Melinda helpfully added, "And Oliver and Gwendolyn could have come this year, too, if only they hadn't extended that ski trip without even telling you, and getting wiped out by that avalanche. I really need another olive." But Melinda was merely staring at her near-empty, now olive-deficient drink without any apparent will to rectify the situation.

"Edna?"

Jim watched while Carol passed the potatoes to Edna, but only after they were interrupted en route by Aunt Gwendolyn who descended upon these white mounds as if they'd been slopes of beautiful snow. At least Gwen was nice enough to smile at Jim. Jim was happy (relatively speaking) to see her there in her red, yellow, and purple ski garb, her face still fashionably sun-burnished red (where precisely did they go these days to ski—could they still go to places like Aspen and Steamboat Springs or even Whitetail?), her demise having affected not a thing physically, it would seem, though spiritually, of course—well, who could say? And it wasn't as if people should be punished eternally for not having called to say they planned to spend the holiday on the slopes, anyway. Plus, as the story went, it was Oliver who had the cellphone on him when the avalanche recovery teams dug them out—too late of course.

Edna was dishing her own potatoes now, as Jim warily eyed the roasted sweet potatoes as they made their way counterclockwise behind the mashed potatoes.

"Well, if there was one thing Oliver was, it was a gentleman." Edna stared fixedly at her daughter while adding, "And if he were sitting here today, he'd still be a gentleman."

Edna passed the potatoes toward her daughter. Jim watched as Oliver, taking his portion, said, "Thank you for the compliment," before passing the bowl to Melinda.

When Jim said, "Don't mention it," Edna said, "Why shouldn't I mention it? It's true, isn't it?"

"Yes," said Oliver, "it is true, isn't it?"

"Not everything you say is true," said Jim, perhaps too testily.

"Jim, are you speaking to me?" asked Edna. "You seem to be looking …"

"It makes me sad to think about these people," Carol interrupted. "Howard and Ellen, Oliver and Gwendolyn."

"And Walter and Lucille," said Melinda. "And Gar—"

This time Carol shook her fork at the young woman. "Don't you dare insinuate a thing about Walter and Lucille. Nothing is going to happen to them just because Lucille has bronchitis and they couldn't come."

Jim was thankful that Carol seemed not to have picked up the name Melinda had been about to mention. At this moment, Jim's perception of the table went like this:

??Gary??	Melinda	Oliver	Edna	Gwen
Jim				Carol
Howard	Empty	Frank	Empty	Ellen

Silently, Jim counted: Carol and himself, Frank and Edna and Melinda, plus these: Howard and Ellen and Oliver and Gwendolyn, yes, there'd still be room for two more next year—but if it was going to be Walter and Lucille like Howard and Ellen and Oliver and Gwendolyn, then they couldn't invite anyone new next year—or might these uninvited guests start sitting on the laps of the invited?

"The Christmas curse, the Christmas curse," chirped Melinda, standing and slowly making her way to the kitchen with her now empty glass.

"I heard that, Melinda." Carol's mood had turned flinty. "This business of Christmas-time spookiness is as false as King Tut's Curse. What if we'd invited you this year and you hadn't come? What do you think would have happened *then*?"

But Melinda was too far gone for this to register, though it had succinctly registered on Edna, who looked none too pleased at the remark.

"As I said," Frank repeated to Jim, "you invite us, we're here—simple as that."

Talk mounted and Jim could see but did not care. What he did care about was that the roasted, non-candied sweet potatoes had now made it around to his end of the table, passed to him personally by Oliver as Melinda, her fourth martini in tow, had not yet retaken her seat. Last year and the year before that and the year before that and the year before that, Gary had been the one who smilingly took his own portion before passing to his father the sweet potatoes with the marshmallow swirl, the boy turning happily nine, then ten, eleven, and twelve. It was the one time of the year Jim could see his son, miraculously still growing, and forever happy with his candied sweet potatoes. This year he would have been able to see Gary as a teenager, but that wasn't going to happen, Jim supposed, because Carol (in the warm pursuit of variety) had decided to change the menu.

How do you rid yourself of unwanted ghosts? Was it too harsh to judge these latecomers as moochers? More importantly: How do you prevent the ghost of a young boy (a ghost, or just a fairly loved image in your mind?) from disappearing? Jim would rather accept them all than lose the one image—his son's—that held meaning.

By seven-thirty Frank and Edna and Melinda had packed each other off and gone home—Edna driving Melinda's car.

"Honestly, at times I wonder," said Carol.

The log fire was low, going out.

"Don't worry. They'll make it home. After all, they're the ones who show up every year." Jim massaged her neck briefly. She tilted her head against his hand. He felt the tension which must have ruled her these past hours.

"Maybe it's me," Jim said reservedly.

"What?"

"Maybe it's me and my resentment. We were so lucky with Gary. Those first few years of trying, and then we had a boy. A fine red-headed boy. Who loved candied sweet-potatoes and baseball and looking in his telescope at the rings of Saturn. We were finally *lucky*. So now we look elsewhere for family, and—it's wrong of me, but for once I'll say it—I resent it when people say they're coming and then they don't. Is that so bad of me? I mean, the fact that I'm irritated can't—cause this, can it? Surely."

Carol placed a palm against the side of her husband's face. "We all want family, Jim. It's only natural." She stroked his hair, but soon he turned to business.

"Maybe we should open our gifts."

Beneath the tree sat the small pile of gifts they pampered each other with at Christmas. Absent Gary, they'd lavished each other with books, sweaters, concert tickets, Sharper Imaginations.

"Jim," she said. Carol seemed to be groping, attempting to formulate her remarks. "It's strange, but I feel as though

I've already had my gift this year. I know I told everyone today that I planned to make the sweet potatoes differently this year, but really, it wasn't a plan at all. This morning, when I realized I couldn't make candied sweet potatoes because I forgot to buy marshmallows, for a moment it felt like someone was watching me. And I don't mean a grown adult. I don't mean to be weird about this. But I remembered how Gary always liked to watch me make the sweet potatoes. And the strongest image—memory, I'm sure I should say—came to mind." She looked closely at her husband. "Could you guess what my greatest gift has been each of these last years without Gary?"

"Won't even try."

"Your vast sense of pleasure when we sit down to Christmas dinner. Every year you smile the happiest smile just as the candied sweet potatoes are being passed to you across that chair where Gary always sat. You'd smile so big it was as if Gary was still here ready for those candied sweet potatoes. Only this year I didn't make them."

But hard against that image, Jim watched a red-headed boy running late to catch a school bus. Then at their door was the dulled face and bewildering stutter of the driver of the truck whose brakes had failed. Jim's mind held eight years of remembered images, all of them better than from that single horrible day, however meager a semblance they constructed of the son who had once breathed and whose spirit had filled the house. But now, only a holiday ritual restored one certain image once a year. It was not a trick that would work a lifetime, but, for now, did that matter?

"Even as a kid, just like Gary, I liked candied sweet potatoes. Still do, truth be known," he told her. "Always will."

He held her tightly, pressing hard against her womb, as if to bring Gary home.

PARA-PET

Within the high parapet that protected the villa's uppermost balcony, the parrot read to Miguel while Miguel peeled an orange, separating it into radiant slices to be eaten one by one. Sunlight reflected off the smooth plastic of Miguel's cellphone on the little table at his side. The brightness made him squint as he contemplated calls to make when the bird took a break. Miguel, of course, was the famous literary artiste Miguel Miguel, the author of seven novels, two collections of short stories, and a slender volume of refined poetry (i.e., not blank verse). Some day, when the two of them had time, Miguel Miguel might also begin scripting dramas. As Miguel was only fifty-two and the parrot twenty-one (red Amazons live into their forties) and both were in sound health, it was not unreasonable to expect fortune would reign long and kindly over Miguel's career.

The parrot (symmetrically named Parrot) "read" (rather than spoke), of course, for it is well known that parrots cannot speak in the sense of consciously propelling forward polite conversation, appropriate, say, to a small dinner party or a soiree—no whip-like witty quips of social repartee. Thus, Parrot might "read" ("recite" was more accurate), though he could not (properly speaking) "speak."

To say the least, Miguel's decorous literary career had been bolstered by his companionship with his dear pet, indeed, in truest terms, his dearest friend. Sixteen years prior, when Miguel's ten-year affair with Clarisse dissolved, she made many common law claims in the nature of property (the in-town condo, heaps of porcelain treasures, and numerous Oriental tapestries). Miguel steadfastly retained, in addition to his seaside villa replete with its lofty parapets, those things which were to him of greatest import: Parrot, along with the substantial and exotic birdcage, reams of wide-lined notepaper and the Mont Blanc pens, plus, naturally, the Smith-Corona portable electric self-correcting typewriter (replaced eventually by a purple-hued MacIntosh due to the difficulty of obtaining typewriter ribbons). [It is noted that the large, gilded cage of which we speak had a diameter of eight feet and was housed permanently in the author's study. The cage was necessary as Parrot's wings had never been clipped. A second, smaller cage was reserved for sunny excursions to the balcony.]

Arguably, it may be said that Miguel's relationship with Parrot had, from the start, been largely foreordained by the fact that Parrot's parroting voice corresponded exactly with the tonalities of Miguel's own voice. Miguel at first had thought of this curious coincidence only in its most obvious practical terms (e.g., giving rote orders to servants, or inviting guests to make themselves comfortable while "I" (the offstage bird) "will be with you momentarily"). Over time more profound and inspirational utilizations were realized, for when Miguel heard Parrot parrot, he heard himself.

The literary relationship began with *Robinson Crusoe* and was greatly amplified in subsequent explorations of extensively varied literary offerings. It was Miguel's habit to read volumes aloud to Clarisse in his study—the same upper room that housed the bird's enormous cage. Here windows opened to sweeping views of the lovely shoreline and permitted as well the pleasantries of morning and evening breezes infused with aromas both delicious and exotic. Miguel noted over time Parrot's immaculate silence and pacific demeanor during the hour or more that the novel was read aloud. Parrot was at that time young and precocious. The parrot's apparent attention contrasted with Clarisse's inattention, as it was her habit to drift into sleep under the extended melodiousness of Miguel's sonorous voice. (In small doses, as when whispered into an ear at bedtime, this voice could also send her into flights of anticipatory copulate ecstasy followed thereafter by impenetrable sleep.) After *Crusoe*, Miguel read in sequence *Wrinkles*, *The Magic Mountain*, *Kappa*, *Catch 22*, *Our Lady of the Flowers*, and works by Melville and Dickens.

We remark that Miguel, who had inherited considerable family holdings, had to this point pursued his literary career chiefly through his professorship at the comfortable little university on his native and rather tiny Caribbean island. He was neither wholly unaccomplished nor immoderately successful. By age thirty-four, he had published a small volume of criticism on the novels of Charles Simmons, written twenty-nine short stories of which five had been published, and lectured extensively on a variety of subjects. Miguel's habit of reading to his mistress began early in their ninth year. Clarisse's beauty—she was eight years his junior—was of such an extraordinary quality as to be attributable to nothing less than ten divinities. He admired her even when she slept beneath the breath of his readings.

In this fashion Miguel's enunciated readings continued book upon book.

One night, satisfactorily fatigued from his bedroom elaborations with Clarisse, Miguel rose from bed at midnight and ambled to his study. He had to prepare a lecture he was to give that week on the use of enjambment in Donne. Rummaging in his desk for notepaper and pen, he suddenly overheard himself talking to himself, a peculiar habit even for a man so insular and removed from common life as Miguel Miguel. (He suffered the effects of cogito-insularity disorder, the addiction to the creative outpourings of one's own mind.) Quite clearly (and oddly) he heard himself speak the following words:

> "An unassuming young man was traveling, in midsummer, from his native city of Hamburg to Davos-Platz in the Canton of the Grisons, on a three weeks' visit. From Hamburg to Davos is a long journey ..."

Miguel continued listening to himself as he unknowingly (apparently) talked to himself, piling words on words. Sumptuous mounds of semantics and syntax! Continuous, on and on he (it) went, hearing himself as he (secretly, even to him) talked to himself. Wonderful words, magical thoughts ... from ...?—but of course! ... H. T. Lowe-Porter's translation of Thomas Mann's *The Magic Mountain*!

He asked himself: Why am I reciting *The Magic Mountain*? He had absolutely no idea. Nor could he fathom *how* such words came to be running, cavorting, indeed leaping through his mind! As suddenly as it started it all stopped. He spoke no more, he heard himself no more. After this quixotic pause (Miguel rubbed his eyes and blinked to rid himself of sleep), he returned to his pen and his notebook and Donne, avowing one thousand words of productive scribbling before giving up for the night. He made excellent progress for the next quarter hour until he once again heard himself speaking:

> "I shall say that he had lace fingers, that, each time he awoke, his outstretched arms, open to receive the World, made him look like the Christ Child in his manger ..."

On and on, a torrent of words. From what book, what mnemonic source? *Our Lady of the Flowers*! Told in such a magnificent, dulcet-toned voice! What a spiritual incantation of Jean Genet's classic!

Suddenly he heard the cage rattle in the small light of the small hours of this otherwise inconspicuous night. Miguel Miguel knew even before he removed the midnight blue carpet from Parrot's cage that the dulcet tones (his own voice!) had been reflected off the surface of a living mirror: his parrot Parrot parroting.

A solid half hour of Genet was followed by a full twenty minutes of Ryunosuke Akutagawa's *Kappa* ("This is a story Patient No. 23 of a lunatic asylum tells anybody he comes across ..."). Miguel, un-jammed from Donne, drained of inner strength, and startled beyond comprehension, threw the night tarpaulin back over Parrot's cage. He returned to bed, worrying fiercely whether he himself might be transforming into Patient 23. At five a.m. he got up again (Clarisse slept peacefully on), ate toast with jam, and proceeded to the study. There he removed the cape from the cage, stared gravely at the parrot (from within, the silence of the tomb), and returned to Donne, whose enjambment he had by the throat in no more than five hours' briskly paced work.

But the curious relationship of man (artiste) and bird (artiste), which had now achieved a certain foothold, was soon destined to take root, mature, and blossom. In those first months, as Miguel's readings continued, Parrot's feats grew ever bolder. Miguel, out of courtesy, moved Parrot's large cage closer to his own reading chair. Thus Parrot perched immediately behind him, while Miguel's lovely mistress graced the divan.

Clarisse continued her habit of sliding into a lethargic state that went ever deeper the more Miguel read. Miguel's first useful discovery was that if he merely waved a book before Parrot's cage, the bird would begin reciting. (Clarisse batted not an eye even when Miguel's Hawthorne shifted abruptly to Parrot's Conrad.)

This observation resulted in Miguel's first strategic change. He began reading to Parrot.

The next discovery was of far greater significance. Late one night, Parrot launched into a recitation of Charles Simmons's *Wrinkles*:

"He learned numbers from his mother before he went to school. First his mother taught the words, which he repeated, unfolding the fingers of his fists one by one ..."

But something tugged at Miguel's critical ear. He raised and lowered his eyebrows, put his hands to his temples. What? *What?*

Scurrying to a bookshelf, Miguel found the book and read:

"His mother taught him numbers before he went to school. First he learned the words, which he said as he unfolded, one by one, the fingers of his fists ..."

During the next two weeks, Miguel often sat befuddled, repeatedly locking his hands together atop his head, as Parrot said: "Ishmael, call me." "It would have been a far greater thing, but someone besides me would have to do it." "Yossarian loved Yossarian." "Shucks, Scarlet."

What was going on here? Errors? Willful mischief?

In six days, Miguel read aloud Arthur Clarke's *Childhood's End*, Clifford Simak's *City*, and Franz Kafka's *The Metamorphosis*.

Within days, the bird parrot-phrased a novella's worth of words that bound together adult humans and a messianic race of aliens in a struggle to save earth's children—who inexplicably were being transformed into grotesquely intelligent, indestructible beings. Encased in impenetrable exoskeletons, these transmogrified children communicated by emitting horrendous pulsating *clicks* at fantastic speeds. The world's children now comprised an enormous supercomputer.

Miguel's hand—furiously transcribing, pen-to-pad, this fabulous bird-garble—cramped. Clarisse (in semi-wakefulness) typed the thirty-thousand-word manuscript. Miguel titled it, *Alien, Cry*. The manuscript was quickly accepted by *Fantasy and Science Fiction* with one minor alteration. Within a year, *Cry, Alien* (*F&SF's* minor alteration) was reissued in a modest-looking Kahlil Gibran-sized volume that (prophetically?) sold thirty thousand copies and placed the name of Miguel Miguel on the outskirts of the known literary map.

Meanwhile, Miguel (and Parrot) had not been standing still. Miguel read aloud many delicious volumes: *Bend Sinister, The Magus, Harmonium, Leaves of Grass, Time and Again* … a mellifluous flow of poetry and fiction.

More and more Clarisse took leave of them to wander the path through the villa's grounds and by the beach. More and more frequently in mid-afternoon she called from the in-town condo professing the need for a nap. She would return the next morning.

Meanwhile Miguel (and Parrot) scrambled through *Alice in Wonderland, Grimm's Fairy Tales, The Hound of the Baskervilles, Innocent Blood*.

They had now read more than fifty books together. The result: two solid novels, *Grey's Club* and *Hawkstern*, plus first impressions for a children's detective story, as yet untitled.

Miguel always authored his own titles. (Would *Cry, Alien* have sold another five thousand copies had it remained *Alien, Cry*?) At first, he checked plotlines and character's names, though he was soon enough convinced that the works could only (and rightfully) be considered original, in the same way a Mickey Spillane murder mystery was original despite the story of Cain and Abel.

McWilliams and Porter of New York began to agent Miguel's novels. For quasi-literary novels they sold well, remarkably so. His portrait appeared on the jacket covers, a tanned, somewhat baby-faced scholar with round widely-set eyes and slightly receding hairline, dressed in a tropical suit, his pose comfortably midway between reclusive genius and man of the people.

Clarisse initiated her legal action to appropriate Miguel's condo and his fine arts possessions shortly after the publication of *Grey's Club*, when it became apparent that the man of letters was starting to achieve national reputation—on his island-nation of some one hundred eighty-five thousand inhabitants. She left while Miguel was in the midst of a six-city U. S. book tour. An expeditious settlement, favorable to Clarisse, put the last ten years behind him. Miguel Miguel—scion of a historically eminent family, incipient literary mogul, patron to a parrot—launched his next literary venture with the bold go-for-broke reading of the gutsy esoteric alongside the masterworks of world literature. Miguel sat in the sun-favored parapet with notepad and Mont Blanc and Smith Corona (and Parrot), and waited for the combinatorial inspiration to take effect.

Parrot authoritatively absorbed, amalgamated, annealed then regurgitated into one a magical mélange of twenty-five illustrious-to-fetid novels. The result was a true *tour de force*—Miguel's greatest work so far, which he proudly titled *The Michelangelo Range*. Within a week of Miguel Miguel's thirty-ninth birthday, *The Range* (as it became known) moved Miguel into the arena of Professionals with Opinions. At his villa he took phone calls from the likes of Jonathan Yardley, Michael Dobson, and John Updike.

Miguel ordered books and more books. He took a six-day excursion to London and Wales, seeking any volume that possessed an intriguing title or auspicious feel. He spent three days in a small town in Texas that reportedly was filled with whole buildings of used books—a report Miguel happily confirmed.

At a dinner party in honor of the mayor of his island nation's capital city, Miguel Miguel hosted in his villa fifty guests of the finest distinction, including the Nobel prize-winning poet DW, whose long-lined poems hauntingly evoked the sun-drenched coasts of scattered Caribbean isles. Miguel Miguel chatted and mingled, emoted and cajoled. At ten p.m., wandering about in a purposeful effort to spread his congenial warmth, he discovered the poet DW in the upper study—where Miguel noted that a servant had neglected to nightcap Parrot in his gilded cage. Thus DW heard (and Miguel heard him hear) the dulcet-toned voice come to life:

"In the inconceivable blight which had become his life, amid the grey evenings which surrounded and fell upon him like the sullen ash of an island volcano, Gideon Grey wept, and forsook his God. No divinity, none, could remove all human dignity, all conceivable grace, leaving a man homeless even of his grief …"

"Look," said the Nobel laureate, "it recites your *Grey's Club*! Whatever have you taught such an intriguing bird…?"

But even at that instant Miguel Miguel was busily crafting the title of his next opus. (Once a project was well underway, Miguel labored assiduously, honing to perfection his latest masterful title—surely the capstone of any work of art.)

The first printing of *Perpetrators of the Vile* numbered one hundred thousand copies. By this time Miguel Miguel was forty-five and at the height of his powers. More printings followed. Movie rights were discussed.

Thus things progressed until this particular afternoon brought Miguel, age fifty-two, to sit on his high balcony absorbing the pleasing radiance of a golden sun. His last slice of orange now finished, his thoughts turned to new worlds to conquer. Six feet away Parrot was perched in the smaller cage while Miguel Miguel on his cellphone commenced an exploratory conversation with his agent, Corey McWilliams of McWilliams and Porter.

"I've been thinking," said Miguel, "mulling it over some time now, actually, how it might be nice to write a play or two." (He began a mental survey of potentially useful dramas: *Man and Superman*, *The Trojan Women*, *Tiny Alice*, *Blithe Spirit*. Were not the possibilities limitless?) "I rather like the appellation 'playwright,' so why should I let it escape me?"

The call to his agent completed, Miguel contemplated whether he should speak to the editor of *This Island Times* concerning his plan to use the university as a forum for fledgling authors to read from works in progress ... with himself, Miguel Miguel, as avuncular host. Miguel smiled contentedly and sucked into his lungs the balmy, sunlit air.

Into the parapet sunlight came now a small dark spot: Navarro, the new and very young servant hired not by Island Condo & Villa-Management Associates but by Miguel himself, appropriating a "target of opportunity" as the Americans put it. A tawny, sinewy youth, with intense dark eyes that admitted of nothing but their vagrant intensity, as a tautology admits a tautology. Miguel Miguel had just last week spied Navarro on the university campus. The lad was followed not ten feet behind by a willowy yet incandescently succulent young woman of incredible beauty. A conversation was taking place, she to him, she to him. The young man was harpooning refuse with a spiked stick. The distance between Miguel and the pair narrowed such that Miguel could at last (and very plainly) distinguish the young man's rebuttal to the girl's entreaties: "Not now, *Clarisse*." Miguel beckoned with a raised arm, and after the shortest of interviews, offered them both immediate employment in his mansion—an offer neither proved able to refuse.

Thus comfortably seated on his balcony on this splendid afternoon, Miguel realized with profound satisfaction that somewhere below, in who knew which room of his estate, this eighteen-year-old nymph was even now dusting the tiger maple cabinets or learning to distinguish the Miles Mason from the New Hall tea services.

It is impossible to say precisely what thoughts Miguel Miguel had had over the years since his own Clarisse pulled up roots. She was now forty-four (presumably a well rested forty-four) while Clarisse II (might she not be?) was as ripe as the original had been at the beginning.

Who knew (not that it mattered) the nature of the existing relationship between young Navarro and the even younger damsel? Had not Miguel Miguel proved that anything was achievable—given the right torque of ingenuity?

"Yes?" said Miguel to Navarro as Miguel punched into his cellphone the number for the editor of *This Island Times*.

"To feed the bird, sir," Navarro answered.

Miguel gestured with his free arm: go right ahead, why don't you?

Miguel listened to the electronic tonalities of the digital phone. Ringing once, twice, thrice. Someone answered, "Natty and Neely Drycleaners." Miguel redialed. A first ring, a second, a third.

Miguel heard the slight bang of the door to Parrot's cage, saw Navarro's back descending the stairs, the task completed.

A fourth ring, a fifth.

Interposed by a detectable tremor from the cage.

Ring six: "Juan Loro, City Desk, Obituaries."

What? Where was the damn editor? "Miguel Miguel for…"

Then the flap of feather and wing. The instantaneous, involuntary redirection of Miguel's eyes. (As of this moment we may imagine Miguel Miguel to have regretted not having clipped Parrot's wings.) The cage! The cage! The door was wide open! Parrot had hopped to the rim of his gilded house—the bird—he—("Oh …!") *flew off*!

The cellphone fell to the serving table between Miguel's chair and Parrot's cage. Miguel himself was on his feet, reaching, grasping, *soaring* in flight for any feather's worth—

Unfortunately, while the voice of Miguel Miguel might fly, his corporeal body could not. In his fall over the precipice (three floors worth) Miguel's gaze remained oddly fixed on the bird—had it not *eloped with Freedom*? Parrot circled, swooped *back* toward the parapet—as there occurred below … an ordinary (albeit weighty) *thud*.

"It was the most amazing thing," exclaimed Juan Loro, the obituary writer at *This Island Times*, shortly after the death had been confirmed. "It is precisely as if he predicted it. I was totally unnerved. A phone call from Miguel Miguel which I had the misfortune to answer. I recognized at once Miguel's singular voice. And to what end, I ask you? That he had fallen off the parapet. 'Miguel Miguel has fallen off the parapet.' Thus did the august author report to me his suicide as though he were speaking of someone else, someone … who had already leapt to his final fate."

Following the state funeral, Corey McWilliams, Miguel's literary agent, scavenged the author's domicile for other writings. He found himself utterly enthralled by the strange parrot's voice—so much so that he found it impossible not to adopt the pet. And during the remaining fourteen years of Parrot's life, McWilliams was astounded to discover that Miguel Miguel had dictated another ten full novels to the bird, which (even more astoundingly) the bird had committed to memory. The parrot recited each in the full richness of the author's voice.

However, as there were no titles, the books were released in the order recited: Posthumous Book I, Posthumous Book II … a final boon to the author of works of such staggering artistic intrepidity.

NATURAL AFFECTIONS

The whitetails weren't too bad this morning. Cindy lost more roses and daylilies out back, but the impatiens survived. Then the foragers loped off, a four-deer family, jumping an old, limp wire fence, marauding somewhere else. Brandon, our 25-month old blond-haired pride, slapped the kitchen windows excitedly, but the brigands were gone. Modern suburbia, as we have come to know it.

"He loves them," she said, sighing as she smiled.

I knew the truce between a sigh and a smile would not last.

"You love them, too, you know," I said.

"But do I love my plants more?" she mock-ruminated, handing me a shopping list. How beautifully seductive was my task mistress.

Cindy traditionally complemented the early peace of Saturday mornings with shopping lists. Milk, one percent (for the two adults); milk, whole (for Brandon); bacon, lean; bananas; cans of pears and peaches; then things Brandon would eat. I didn't examine the remainder—the list was short—my mind was elsewhere. Cindy didn't know it, but I had an errand of my own.

I cranked the Ford F-150 up and revved the engine for Brandon to hear from the house. That's the way bears growl, I'd told him. A child's fascination with animals vs. an adult's preoccupation with the problems animals caused. Were deer as pretty as the flowers they ate? I liked deer and flowers and Cindy. Brandon liked deer. But someday soon Cindy would ask me to put in a new, higher fence—we'd already tried spraying deer repellent. That new project would be the end of Brandon's love affair with deer, unless I could convince my fair lady to try deer-resistant plants, my last fence-avoidance option.

I put the pickup into reverse. Candlewood was a fifty-year-old development, built when builders still left trees on lots, each lot one-half to a full acre. Ours was three-quarters, nicely landscaped, right down to the long gravel driveway I carefully backed out onto Longwood Road which led to Raven.

Soon I was on Old Route 14. Route 14, toward Hendrix, our hometown, drove straight at the heart of this mostly green state. An old but growing city at the foot of lush mountains, Hendrix beckoned ten miles away, not that I was headed that far. Road crews were widening 14, turning it into a four-lane highway. Hendrix as it was didn't need another highway of course, but trees were falling even in our neighborhood, squeezing new houses into hitherto secret but unfortunately not after all imaginary spaces. Elsewhere, in newly carved landscapes, the trees laid flat as troops preparing to do pushups. Along both sides of Route 14, billboards fronted phalanxes of backhoes and bulldozers, proclaiming the coming of Vermillion Estates, Huntington Village, Leland Lake Homes. Tennis, golf, restaurants, cinemas, shopping malls. Odd to think that Hendrix had been founded as a mountain springs spa; that it still held an annual water-tasting contest courting entries worldwide.

Grady's Grocery, two-plus miles from home, was just opening as I pulled in. Bill stood just outside, wrestling with his moose.

"Will this get me a discount?" I asked, offering help.

Bill Grady was your basically large economy-size person, his big, meaty face rightly distinguished by his boxer's nose, twice-broken. He had a big gut but solid, and a lineman's shoulders. "Look, I need help with the backend. I got the front just fine."

Even stuffed, the animal was heavy. I pushed as much as lifted.

"I'm planning on fixing it permanently out front, just haven't got around to it yet." He stood back to admire it. "Whadd'ya think?"

"Handsome creature," I said. If he was really planning on anchoring it, as in cement, I wondered how the hide would smell on a rainy day. "Beats a cigar store Indian," I constructively added. What do you tell someone who'd shot a moose in his parking lot? It was obviously illegal to discharge a firearm in a commercial zone, but Emmett & Wilkins already had a stuffed black bear sitting in front of their hardware store, and they weren't woodsmen. Only two weeks ago in Hendrix, as documented for TV by the store's security cameras, a bear cub had followed a woman into a dress shop just as if the cub had been imprinted to follow tall ladies in yellow dresses. The city council had begun discussing tranquilizer guns.

"A bull moose is dangerous, you know," Grady added. "A moose in the wild, a big one, is an imposing animal."

"Yeah, Bill. I'm impressed. It makes you think, what next. Well, I got my chores," I said, holding up Cindy's shopping list.

"Earl, you go right on in." He'd already turned to the next on-comer. "Whadd'ya think?" I heard him say, slapping the animal's backside.

The grocery list wasn't enormous, and I was done in maybe four minutes.

"Hi, Mr. Pearson," said Billy Jr., manning checkout.

"What's he going to do with the next moose that crashes town?" I queried.

"Actually," said the boy, scanning bar codes, "he'd like more. Old Will Hooper's gonna get rich."

"Um," I said. Will Hooper, until recently our occasional taxidermist, was now a man with a prospective future.

"Well, as long as they don't go the way of the Dodo," I said, taking my bag.

"Dodo?"

He hadn't a clue. "Read your Charles Darwin," I advised.

"Not much for reading, Mr. Pearson. We got HDTV now."

Nobody had ever figured Billy Jr. was exactly college material. He didn't have the wide plane of shoulders, the ornery bulk of his old man.

Chores accomplished, I drove to Ward Dressler's to check progress on my secret project. Dressler Trail was an old road guarded by pines and poplars and a low, neglected wall of stone. Ward lived a secluded life on property until recently equally secluded. Now of course that low wall might be on someone's eradication plan. But Ward had thirty-six acres and an old coot's tenacity.

I parked where the gravel road ended short of his house. With milk in the truck, I didn't plan to stay long.

Ward was an early riser, a man who kept pace with the sun.

"A watched pot sometimes boils," he said, opening the door before I could knock. Ward's matchstick eyebrows alternately rose and fell welcomingly—a nervous tic. He was a hunch-shouldered man with no discernable lips. As gravity took over with age, he'd gained a turned-down mouth, but I knew his smile resided in his eyes.

We shook hands and he waved me in.

"I shouldn't do this, you know. It's too early in the day for good light," he said. Ward lived in a modest house with one grand exception—the cavernous studio he'd long ago built off the back. It paid homage to what Ward valued—light. Even now as we entered his high-ceilinged "chapel"—the name he facetiously applied to his studio—a calming shaft of natural light fell through tall chalet-style windows, capturing his seemingly forever draped easel. Looking toward the outside world, the windows framed a large field touched by pines ascending a mountainous slope. The sun was just beginning to clear the trees. In another hour, I knew, the light would form a gentle beam in the motes that floated in this room, something indistinct but perceptible, like mist from a waterfall.

Every wall of the house held examples of Ward's grand and sometimes moodily evocative landscapes—mountains and timberline lakes; tumble-down cabins held in dim forest break light or the silent embrace of winter snow; isolated churches and neglected cemeteries; automobiles junked at defunct gas stations. Elsewhere, like some strange form of litter, numerous canvases—possibly errant or unfinished—leaned against the walls, their faces turned, hidden. I first noticed perhaps nine or ten of these hidden paintings when I visited two weeks before. Now, there was twice the number.

Amid this jumble of canvases, Ward approached the one on the easel. This single canvas centered my attention.

"Your wife got any idea yet?" he asked.

"Nope. None at all."

"Well, I warned you I'd take my time. Though, God knows, it's seldom enough someone actually commissions me to paint anything. I'm not exactly a portrait artist, you know. Landscapes," he said, jerking a thumb at the walls, "my preference." It was his familiar I-don't-do-portraits lecture, still unchanged.

I stared at the canvas, transfixed. I must have sighed.

"Well, I hope that's not a sigh of regret," he commented.

It was beautiful. Incomplete but without a hint of blemish. Rosy pastoral in color, two bodies indistinctly

separate, indistinctly one. My Cynthia, my Brandon, alive
on canvas.

"Want coffee?"

I nodded without even thinking.

Ward disappeared into his walk-in closet-sized kitchen.

I stepped back from the painting. Wasn't it beautiful
from any perspective?

Yes, of course, he'd have preferred to do a real life portrait,
but I'd given him a photo, in fact a series of photos, in order
to maintain surprise—our third anniversary coming. Good
art took time, I supposed. And wasn't this promising?

I walked about unconsciously, looking from this
distance, examining from that angle, from any vantage
point to confirm prospective beauty.

Yes.

Though in a way, it did seem the painting hadn't changed
a great deal from when I'd looked at it two weeks ago. Come
to think of it, how long should a good portrait take? Did I
have any real idea? Was three months unreasonable to be at
this stage, good in feeling, good in promise, but yet … still
an incomplete promise?

I turned as Ward reentered the room handing me my
coffee. Then, in my turning, just out of the corner of my eye,
as though noticing a lesion in the light streaming through
those tall windows, I saw.

"Ward, do you know you've got a red fox out there on
your lawn?"

"Probably after the turkeys."

"Turkeys?"

We approached his window.

"Next we'll have pumas back. Won't that be something,"
he said and laughed. The fox moved on.

Outside, a faint cloud was slowly passing, yielding a
trace of darkness. The change in light drew my eye to other
corners of the room. The hodgepodge of canvases leaning
here, propped there, turned to the wall, the incognitos.

As if a peeping Tom, I turned my head, nearly twisting my neck, to examine one. Now I saw it looking back at me from the canvas: that very fox, vivid. I looked at Ward quizzically. I turned another canvas. Two frolicking foxes, steel gray. On a third canvas, a pristine quail, shimmering fat in mottled colors. Again: A toy-size animal, the mercurial chipmunk, stock-still, but poised for a darting run. Again: A plain, ordinary 'possum, staring back as if into a lens. Another: A blacksnake swollen in its middle by a meal. Next, two giant stags locking horns, combat raucous. I kept turning canvases. A field consumed with cavorting rabbits. Elsewhere: wide-eyed owls, wing-dipping barn swallows, shining purple martins. Tentative: an osprey, I think. Without reservation: an American bald eagle.

I turned to my portrait artist, the slow and patient recluse.

He blushed, then regained his poise. I felt a great unease.

"Why don't we just drink our coffee by the light?" he said, drawing to the window two modern lawn chairs comfortably crafted with all weather fabric. He placed a small table between us for our coffees.

We both sat for maybe three minutes watching while wildlife traversed or stopped and peered our way. Were we on display?

I decided against making a direct assault.

"Is this common, Ward? An entourage like this?"

"That's precisely the word, 'entourage.' Entourage for my awaited puma, maybe!" He chuckled at the likelihood. "I think what I've got is a roadway of a kind."

Looking, I spotted small squirrels heading for trees, running up and around them, charging headfirst up and down after each other.

"Wouldn't it be fun to play like that?" he said.

I studied him as if he himself were a portrait I'd never before seen. These new paintings—animals, all—looked

finished, while my family's remained—a fantasy? We
frankly studied one another. It didn't take clairvoyance to
see my sudden doubts. His body seemed to sag.

"To tell the truth, Earl, I've been a little distracted
lately, I guess you could say." He paused, sipped his coffee.
"Normally, I'd never have considered your idea for a portrait.
But I started. Up to then, didn't have much confidence I
could paint a living thing, something that didn't hold just
as still as the earth—a good old landscape. Not that you
could call two faces in a photo, what you gave me to paint
from, something truly alive. No offense, Earl. You've heard
they're gonna renovate the old Wyatt Bottling Factory?
Convert the whole thing to art studios, draw more attention
to downtown Hendrix. I was actually considering it. Then
… things changed."

He rose from his chair, hunted among the wall-turned
paintings, and brought one back, which he proudly
displayed. A *water buffalo?*

"Found one in *National G*. Who knows, I might become
a naturalist. Ever see the movie *Fargo,* where the artist's bird
gets picked for the three-cent stamp?"

"Ward, that's fine … But I've got an anniversary in
another month."

Ward's eyes blinked in the cloud-softened light. I
watched him nod. "How 'bout I freshen that coffee?"

I acquiesced for the sake of civility.

"So," he said, returning with two freshened mugs,
"Truth is I've become sort of obsessed. Addicted, even. Been
living out here all these years and, until Hendrix turned into
a developer's paradise—you know they've plumb cleared
all the trees for hundreds of acres just a quarter mile down
the road—I never saw the like before. … You ever been
addicted to anything?"

"You're telling me you're now a sucker for quails?"

"Quails, foxes, Lord knows, I've got the Ark's cargo on
parade out here. And of course you'll say a quail's part of

nature's own, and that naturally your wife and son take dominion over quails. And, Lord indeed, you got a pretty wife and it's sure not easy to explain why I'm not attending the image of your pretty wife rather than—"

"A water buffalo?"

Ward didn't wince. He continued to look out the window, and sipped from his mug. "Fair shot, Earl. Not below the belt." Then he looked up. "And there. Our common, pretty friends," he said.

In the distance four deer showed, looking uncertainly at the house before dallying. I wasn't about to assume they were the same four from our place.

"Deer everywhere nowadays," he said. "People, too. What an amazing mix."

Momentarily, the topic provided a peaceful diversion. "Deer," I said, nodding. "We're overrun with 'em. Cindy's had it. They're killing her landscaping. Sprays don't work. I'm fixing to try deer resistant plants next. Now, she wants me to build a fence."

Ward nodded knowingly. "Deer resistant plants won't do the job. You'd have to replace all the plants you've got, and the new ones aren't foolproof. Chrysanthemum. Supposed to be deer-proof. Deer won't eat the plant, but they will eat the blossoms, and that's all people care about. Trust me, deer are like goats, but prettier. And as for prettiness, not a bad second to a family portrait—an exaggeration, but … As for fences, a deer can leap an eight-footer. Rare, but true. Fence would be your best bet, but you'd better make it seven feet, and it'll alter your view. What we really need is fewer deer. But they're smart. They adapt. They actually like suburbia, I'm learning, especially islands of grass or bushy thickets near woodland. They'll eat what you grow, fall back into the woods. They learn your habits, visit when you're out. They get healthier, even. Does start having *more* fawns. Population goes up. Contraceptives either don't work or wear off."

This was all news to me. Coffee and a lecture. "So what's the recourse?"

"Culling. But they learn about that, too. A deer sees enough deer stands, it learns what to avoid. What you need to take out is the does. Or go build your tall fence. If I may wager a guess, Cindy's going to end up with her fence."

A nice discussion, perhaps, but in the end I had to ask what he was going to do.

"Finish your painting if I can," he said. "Time's not the issue. There's time. You've got the bond of a handshake … and money's been passed. I'm not one to renege. Not finishing a job's disrespectful, and besides, you're good people. I can still visualize Cindy as a child, you know. I used to fish with her daddy. I can visualize her quite well as a child, actually, back when she *liked* deer …"

He turned silent.

"But are you addicted to this other thing?" I queried. "If you're addicted … I don't want to lose your friendship, Ward. And I want to make my wife happy."

He stood when I stood. His smiling eyes were still smiling and just as friendly when I turned to leave, but that word 'addiction' unnerved me. *Was* his word his bond?

"Oh, good," said Cindy when I got home. "You bought milk. I wondered if I'd forgot to mark it." (Actually I'd returned to the store and bought new, replacement milk, worried that I'd left the milk out longer than intended at Ward's.) Brandon was tottering across the kitchen floor, like a boy learning to walk on stilts, trying to catch up to one of his 'bots, a toy fireman wandering off.

Cindy put the groceries away.

Then in an instant I saw her face flush. "Everything here but Brandon's animal crackers," she said. "You know how he is without them." She bravely smiled, though she was right about Brandon's animal crackers.

I could survive the animal crackers as a poor joke (on me), but actually it opened a new opportunity in task management.

At Wilmer's Landscapes, Bud Wilmer suggested five deer-holdout plants, three of which I walked off with. Not forgetting the animal crackers, I arrived home to ask Cindy where I should plant the deer-proof trophies. I admitted it was an experiment. So the afternoon went to planting and mulching and watering.

That evening we sat in the back sunroom, keeping an eye on Brandon and an eye on the world outside.

I asked Cindy what she thought of the animal explosion we were experiencing.

"Love-hate, I suppose," she said. "Sara Gilford would like to put Depends—those adult diapers—on the geese that have settled their pond. They're so pretty and the flyovers are wondrous but when they land and settle ... And the deer are certainly pretty. But it's not just their eating habits, there's Lyme disease. They talk about an overpopulation of deer and an extended hunting season and I wonder how safe we are out here at times with buckshot flying even though hunters are supposed to keep their distance. And what about fox and raccoons? What about rabies? You hear about rabid raccoons, don't you?—and Brandon can't outrun a raccoon. He might even approach one." She watched Brandon momentarily while she rocked in her rocking chair, her favorite chair in the house. "Yet, it's becoming like an open zoo almost, these days. In a way, it's wondrous. Are we crowding them out? Are we going to have to turn everything into parks to protect them? It's almost nice, conceptually. After a while, you feel you've seen it all but elephants and mountain lions ... So, it's not quite magic—yet."

Ward called three weeks later and said he had a gift, courtesy of his new laptop and some software.

When I arrived in late morning he asked whether I wanted the white or the red.

"... or red what?"

"Wine, you idiot." I could see he was bravely smiling. I chose the red.

"Now," he said, ushering me into his studio.

There she was, Cindy, a three foot by three foot *photograph* at the height portraits are to be hung, taped to the inside of the studio window. A two-foot border of plain brown shopping paper framed the photo.

Ward, holding his glass of white, asked, "Recognize it?"

I stared, befuddled. "It's one of the photos I gave you to work from. You've blown it up."

"Of course I have."

I approached it and raised a finger as if to touch it. "It's very grainy."

"Of course it is. You blow up a five-by-seven inch photo to this size, and it's not going to retain detail."

"Well, won't that affect the quality of the portrait?"

"Not if I'm painting from the five-by-seven and using that blow up to keep my mind focused. Mounted up there on the windows, she's like part of the woodlands, except she's a perfect still life. None of my pets will do that for me."

"What the hell?" I said, slightly confused.

"In effect, consider the blow up the view from my 'deer stand,'" he said. "If I ever look at the window, I see nothing but Cindy—I've got a five-foot square image blocking half my window … I'm animal-*deprived* right now, I don't see anything but that photo if I stare at my window—all so I remember I'm supposed to be working from *this*." He held the five-by-seven-inch photo between two fingers and shook it. "Ready for a toast?"

"I hope to God I am," I nervously assented.

Ward pulled the photo blow up down from the window. Light filled the room. He turned, indicating with an extended hand the covered easel to our backs. Now the light fell on it. Without theatrics, he lifted the cloth.

Once again I was in love with my beautiful wife and speared in the heart by my young son. The canvas I had believed this artist capable of painting stood before me.

Ward proudly sipped from his glass of wine; I was too absorbed by this gift of light and color and detail to drink.

"The detail," I said.

"Not exactly Impressionism, is it? I'm fast in the grasp of all those Post Office bird stamps. Detail and realism to the hilt. I've thrust the sword in it, absolutely! They're as good as … I wager … any wildlife portrait you'd find on the market. I think all my practice with water buffaloes has rather made this my …"

He seemed about to say the word "masterpiece," to which conclusion I leaped by saying, "Yes." And quite happily paying the balance.

"**B**ut why didn't you have yourself put in?" Cindy stared in awe at the portrait almost a full two minutes before picking this nit.

I couldn't have explained it to her satisfaction and didn't try.

And of course she was the one to notice the painting hanging on the background wall of the canvas. That is, the painting contained within her portrait, the smaller portrait of a fawn and a young child, a pretty, pigtailed girl, caught in the subtext of the grander portrait, the diminutive background image making its own minor ray of light.

"That's odd, but nice. I wonder why he did it, particularly when it's hardly noticeable. You don't think he means anything by this, do you?"

Finally, I offered a casual note, "He knew you, you know… as a child. He knew your dad. Maybe he remembered—"

"That I wore pigtails?"

"Maybe even that you liked deer."

"You don't think he could have something else in mind? Could he be saying our next child will be a girl? Is he prone to making predictions?"

I considered his predictions about deer culling that did not concentrate upon does. Not that I said anything.

"Don't prejudge," Cindy added. "Admit it's possible."

Children and wives are darling, but expensive. So I smiled warmly and said, "It's…"

THE SOCIAL COMPACT

I met him in a coffee shop. Nothing fancy, a smudge: Klinger's Café. Solvents for the Soul, its signboard said. An oddity anywhere else, but not in this part of town, where nothing kept shape but the darkness.

Outside it was dead-winter cold. I'd turned my collar up. My feet clicked against December's grey slate of street. Hands in pockets, my breath steaming like the soul of coffee itself—then rattling overhead, this solicitous sign, a siren in wind. Solvents for the Soul, indeed. Not Solutions, not— even better—Indulgences. But I had no business rewriting it even for amusement's sake. Doctor's orders.

Tinkling of doorbell as I stepped inside. Dwarf-sized shop, rent presumably anemic: Five Formica-topped tables, three with customers. Two ratty-looking booths, their once semi-plush cushions long ago squeezed flat by the heft of donut dunkers. Both occupied, one by a stout and grungy twosome, the second by a man with his face buried under hunched shoulders, an innocuous grey head.

Young lad behind the counter: twenty-one or -two, white-smocked, flush-cheeked, a mild but honest-looking smile. Behind him a blackboard fashioned the "Solvents" by geography: Roman Forum, Parisian Culture, British Biscuit, others, each bearing small, semi-legible chalk-work scribbles meant to convey this or that quality, "baldy obstreperous," "sumptuously seductive;" you get the idea—pretension in a dive.

Buenos Aires Cappuccino Collegial, my first request, was unavailable: the cappuccino machine needed mending; they'd asked a month ago, but repair was regrettably slow. They did have Greenwich Candelabra, however. "It tastes pretty much like tiramisu," the boy advised.

"Just what I want at nine a.m.," I said, "dessert." When he looked at me uncertainly I added, "Yes, yes, that'll be fine." Two dollars, but with half-price refills. "And the coffee cake, too, please."

I took a table close to the front, a chair obliquely facing the window. I now effectively presented my back to everyone in the room except the loner in the front booth, who also faced the window. My choices (besides eat and drink) were to (1) read someone's discarded business section of the newspaper (others were similarly reading what may have been a communally shared paper), (2) stare past the fog of winter sunlight caught in its transit of grimy window, or (3) errantly look at the man in the booth, who, from my vantage, sat in profile.

The business news was certainly an option, as these days it carried not only the staid quotes of Ups and Downs, but photos of the occasional handcuffed billionaire, or sprightly tales of the nouveau-chic niche market in personal body armor, or the cheekiness of nanotechnology futures.

I swear to you I had been sipping my lamentable Oreo mousse with the paper laid flat, reading only this or that article, when from his booth the gentleman (call him that: my age and attired in a suit, though not fashionable, its delicate but tedious lines of lime laid longitudinally upon a tired, shiny-with-age blue serge) addressed me:

"You're knowing me."

I looked up. "Pardon?"

"You're knowing me, yes? Please."

Pattern recognition is one of the lovelier arts of the human soul: to see something, or part of something, and fill it in, to complete wholeness where there had in fact been a hole in comprehension. As I said, I'd seen this man only in profile — the left side of his face; I'd read with the paper lying flat on the table, my eyes focused on paper, my brain consuming only stories of venture capital and insider trading — this man's visage being nothing more to me than a bland peripheral grey quadrant of no distinction whatsoever. I'd found only my coffee regrettable, not him. Yet here he was rotating his face into play, rotating his soul into my span of attention. And this, I saw, changed everything.

I hesitated. "I'm sorry, I don't follow." A defensible answer.

The man merely looked, leaving his remark incomplete. His eyes were large and quiet: perfectly round, motionless orbs, black as coffee. But these dark eminences were unnervingly displaced, their arrangement unnatural. I stared back as long as I could, to show my innocence, my lack of understanding, his inescapable misunderstanding. Any accusation was quite his own: that was what my look said. We waited, two uncertain quantities — he would back down. But yet he looked.

"Sorry," I said finally, returning to the page.

Still he would not give up.

"Please. For the honor of your presence." It was now impossible not to look. He had extended an arm, his palm up, toward the unoccupied side of his booth. "Sit."

He calmly waited. I realized in fact there was a courtliness in his manner of defiance, if that is what it was. In theory I could choose belligerence, taking his forwardness as the true insurrection.

But how to deny *him*?

The ordinary tools were not, I found, available.

"Well," I said, rising, "this is kind of you, though I shall soon —"

"Yes, but coffee on a morning such as this is always such a pleasant thing," he said, rising as if to escort me to the seat.

"As you see, mine will soon be gone," I said, practically forcing him to examine my cup as I nonetheless took the proffered seat.

"Ungodly," he said, inhaling with intense disfavor. "You have been given their horrible sweet. They do have some good coffees, but you have not been well advised."

I carefully examined his statement for some hidden implication. "Well, the young man certainly seems to be trying to help."

I watched as the man ironically smiled. "Believe me," he said, "I shall not call him a cretin."

To smile at that remark would have been utter cruelty. But to look away would have been just as cruel. The best that could be hoped for was to maintain composure.

He widened his smile as if inviting me to look at him. There was, therefore, nothing for it but to look.

I would not lightly apply the word cretin to any soul. I would like to think I would not apply the word under any circumstance—though I know with confidence that I, like all men, lie when lying is the only thing to do.

"Let me improve your fortune," he said. "I take you for a man who appreciates subtlety."

"As do I you." A politic reply—any wariness but human.

"Only a moment," he said, and rose from the table. He carried himself with a graceful gait across the room, leaned into the young man, and spoke quietly. In a minute he had returned, a cup of coffee in each hand.

"Please," he said. "This will be an improvement."

I had to admit it was. But when I asked what coffee it was, he said nothing.

"Your cake," he said after an interval, "it is good?"

"Yes, quite good."

"Even though it is not best for the waistline, eh?"

He smiled quite grandly this time, exposing his bottom row of teeth in a way that was not to his advantage. From one side of his mouth to the other, his teeth curved inward, a concavity on its way to collapsing. But what he meant, of course, was that he was a thin man, while I …

"From behind, as I am walking, as I make my way down a sidewalk, as I cross a garden path, I know in its proportions my body betrays nothing, nothing whatsoever. I am in fact, quite the rake. Would you believe it?"

I pondered diplomacy.

"I, as you see, cannot speak of my own waistline."

"Ah—however, does that prevent you from speaking of mine?"

Again, the clever grin which broke upon the crevice of the corrected cleft palate: the impertinence of the concentrically shuffled teeth.

"Doesn't modesty prevent your asking such a question?" But why hurt the man?

Once again, he only smiled. "One should be modest where appropriate. One should be thankful where appropriate. One should be honest in—so far as possible— every transaction at hand."

In effect, he'd acknowledged that at times truth was a boundary to be crossed.

I sipped and when I did not sip I sometimes stared. It was undeniable that I stared. It was undeniable, too, that he took some strange satisfaction in my staring, as if my staring permitted him to see frailness in the psyche of ordinary man.

No doubt I did not flinch in bolstering his perception of weakness in others, if that was what his own psyche required. Perhaps this even *made his day.*

Yet he seemed so wholly a gentleman, and so wholly unfortunate.

"Well," I said, "I have finished. It was good. What coffee was it?"

Again, his examining look. "I will tell you that tomorrow, if you would be so good as to return."

Here I had him. "All I need do is ask at the counter what coffee you ordered."

"Of course," he agreed. "Or perhaps I requested two different coffees, in which case you could not be certain. I would hope such a small mystery impels your return so that I may again enjoy your company."

I rebutted, "I already owe you for this. Two dollars?"

He raised a finger along the right side of his nose, as if he were about to make a point. "I told him you were new and to treat this as a refill. Just give me one dollar—forget the tax, it's only a nuisance—and I will satisfy your coffee curiosities if you but permit me a little game."

Of course, the issue of the coffee was really unimportant, but I assented and paid him, knowing full well he had no power to hold me to any "agreement" I didn't like.

He proceeded, "I have formed the opinion that you and I are the same age. *Precisely* the same age. Surely you must agree this is possible; I am convinced it is fact. My grey hair, your grey hair. The way our eyebrows have grown unruly and merge like colliding galaxies. And the little tufts which inhabit our ears—which prudence demands we occasionally trim. I shall not begin to assess other facial characteristics as to do so in my case would be unseemly. But my game will prove we were born on the same day."

His eyes gleamed—even so, what was there to lose? "All right. A game."

"Yes, but we must play it my way. You must agree to that."

Again I assented.

"I shall state your age and the year of your birth. If I am correct, you shall then tell me which quarter of the year you were born in. I shall then declare the month in which you were born. You shall then disclose the week in which you were born. I shall then furnish the day."

A parade of hoops, in other words.

"If we're going to do it that way, why not guess which sign of the Zodiac you or I was born under? Or why go to all this trouble—why not just compare drivers' licenses?"

"Please. You agreed to my rules."

Ah, the sanctity of the social covenant: "Okay. Your way."

He immediately said, "You are fifty-two." Then he named the year.

He was correct but I was nearly ebullient at this point, as my age was closer by far to fifty-three. Perhaps he sensed eagerness on my part. Perhaps I had inadvertently disclosed information.

"Yes. Yes, that is the year." I sensed he would again coyly smile, but he did not. "So now, under your rules, I am to tell you the quarter of the year in which I was born."

"That is correct. The quarter of the calendar year. Not the fiscal year. Not the season."

I shrugged. "The first quarter of the year, then."

"Meaning either January, February, or March, in other words."

"Yes, 'in other words.'"

"Please, just confirm it for me. Repeat so that I can confirm your understanding. I do not want you to slip out on a technicality."

"Oh, very well. 'January, February, March.' Yes."

"January," he said, without hesitation.

He was correct. He was indeed correct. He'd nearly pounced with his answer. An uncanny cunningness? He seemed on the one hand aberrant, physically aberrant, yet ornately human beneath his threadbare cloth of skin. How much of him was guile?

"January," he repeated. "Admit it."

"Of course," I said, smiling. Surely, there was a joke to this. "Yes, January."

"I am pleased to hold your attention."

"Yes—yes …" I admitted, nodding agreement.

"To remind you: the next obligation is yours, to name the week in January."

"But how shall we define a week?"

"By starting with January first as the first day of the first week of the month."

"Then …" Suddenly I saw a fallacy in my confidence. "Well, to be honest, the fifth week."

"You are certain?"

"Well, don't you *know*—if our birthdays are the same—surely you already know!"

"The thirteeth—*ahhh…*"

"Ha!" I cried out.

But now I saw that he had been stifling a sneeze. "The thirty-*first*," he finished. "We were both born on the thirty-first of January, fifty-three years ago next month."

I wanted to call him on it. "It was a guess. It was a guess!"

"But you admit I was correct. We were born on the same day. If not for DNA itself, we could be twins."

"It was a guess. That is all that it was. I'll show you my driver's license—"

"A condition that is not necessary. If you had said you were born, let us say, on the twenty-ninth of January, *I* would not have challenged you. I might have concluded you were prevaricating, but I would not have challenged you."

I held my wallet. "Here, here …" I fumbled for my license.

He raised a hand. "A gentleman does not." He placed his hand quietly on top of mine, closing the wallet, effectively bringing the matter to an end.

It had been a simple game, but where a minute ago I'd felt amusement, I now felt disheartened and diminished by it.

"Please," he said, "believe me. We are the same. You and I. We are the same."

I was too exhausted to speak.

"My name is Venus Magnum. I shall again be here tomorrow. I invite you to join me. This booth is quite my own. And the coffee—indeed, even the cake if you like—shall be on me." He rose, donned top coat and scarf, tipped his hat first to me, then to the boy behind the counter, and walked, almost gallantly, through the door, into the brace of a mid-December day.

The day turned colder, even more blustery. I judged blustery to be in perfect keeping with my experience at the coffee shop. I wandered some eight or ten aimless blocks before returning to Emory Bergen's (yes, the prize-winning novelist's) frumpy apartment, closeted my wraps, and sank within the amply upholstered armchair that faced the book-littered couch. A mini-tower of books also crowned the hassock while even more had made a land grab on the coffee table. At the moment, I wanted nothing to do with the ninety books I'd agreed to read as surrogate for one of the three jurors on this year's panel of judges for the Wilson Walker Prize in American Letters.

I thought of a musical piece: *Kinderszenen*: Scenes from childhood. That is what billowed in my mind—the incoherent past stirred by the provocative ministrations of this grey-headed conductor with the ridiculous name 'Venus Magnum'—he'd raised within me the grey ashes of my own childhood scenes. My recollections of childhood were not of the soft quality of *Kinderszenen*, the surpassing and delightful melodies composed by the disconsolately romantic Robert Schumann. Mine were a blight.

Surely my morning's interlocutor—a disfigured male with the ill-proffered name 'Venus'—was some kind of charlatan.

At age thirty-one, I had once paid two dollars to an amusement park attendant whose job it was to guess my age, within one year, and my weight, within two pounds.

Though she misjudged my weight (she mercilessly gave me four unwanted pounds), she told me I was thirty-one without a moment's hesitation. I have felt ever since that it is not such a challenge to assay an individual's age.

Not for a moment did I believe Venus Magnum and I shared the same birthday. Charity didn't demand gullibility, did it? It was enough that I'd been asked to believe a man's name could possibly be Venus Magnum. But chicanery aside, there was something uncanny about the whole business.

It began with Venus Magnum's asymmetrical face but it did not stop there. It ran from his bisected face—one-half blandly normal, the other a malignancy—to things that had nothing to do with him, but only with me.

On April first of the year I turned nine, my mother deposited me with an aunt, drove off, and never returned. My aunt Lila said my mother had left because she'd finally located my father somewhere near Phoenix. Our family was to be reunited, I'd been optimistically told. But I had never met my father and that was the last I was ever to see of my mother.

My mother had always told me I would never be truly alone in life because I carried within me my twin brother. "Within you," she said, "you carry your brother Nevus, who is your twin." Her concocted explanations were legion. "When I was pregnant with you, Altus, I was also pregnant with Nevus. The doctor showed me the ultrasounds—Altus and Nevus. Your father and I named both of you even before you were born." Whenever I asked where Nevus was, she repeated: "Within you." If I asked *where* precisely within me and how he got there, the answers varied. "He is your hearts-blood" was one answer. Or she would dodge and divert the question. "Later the doctors lied," she explained. "They lied that I had a twin?" "No," she answered, "they lied that there was *not* a twin. But brothers do not just disappear, no matter what the doctors say." In a later edition, she asserted that not only had the doctors lied, but that they knew where

Nevus was—that he was with my father, that the doctors knew where that was, but wouldn't admit it. Yet still she insisted my brother was within me, or part of me, no matter what. When I turned six I was enrolled in school as Altus Nevus Grande. "There," she said to me. "Your name is the proof that you are two good boys in one."

On my twelfth birthday Aunt Lila said it was time for me to be told the truth. "You had a brother, but he was deformed and did not live." "Deformed in what way?" "Very badly deformed." But I wondered whether my father had secretly raised Nevus and my mother had run off to join them in Phoenix. "Could we have been Siamese? Is that it? Did Nevus die when they tried to separate us?"

I think I have spent most of my life in the role of Odysseus, hunting not Penelope but the inestimable Cyclops. And like Cyclops, my life has passed before me half invisible.

Venus, indeed. Magnum, indeed. Surely this man knew: Nevus, not Venus; Grande, not Magnum. He had to be a scholar of some sort. He read literary magazines. Or had I been depicted in the arts section of a newspaper he'd ferreted at Klinger's Café? Occasionally diminutive bio-snaps appeared on the subject of Altus Nevus Grande. I was the onetime novelist felled at an early age, after courteous but innocuous reviews of his first, short, "potentially promising" novel—laid lame by a stroke at thirty-three. Surely heft of heart (mine was enlarged) had never aided my health—and if Nevus was my hearts-blood, a transfusion would not have been objectionable.

So when I could no longer create, I explicated the creations of others. Like the unfortunate poet Reetika Vazirani, I became eternally itinerant, campus-hopping, never tenured, never secure, never complete. I had friends, but no saviors. The more I moved, the more acquaintances replaced my friends, the more obsessively obnoxious I became as a critic. I freelanced book reviews for the *Baltimore Sun* and the *Washington Post*. Out of perversity I often wrote bad reviews for what I truly considered good books—the reverse of a stock analyst touting one stock publicly, while calling it "a dog" privately. I admit to the sins of jealousy, ill-will, distemper. I wrote favorably of John Fowles, a writer, like me, abused by stroke.

I freelanced not only writing, but OxyContin, too—the Nevus inside me being my sole consumer. Eventually I freelanced a suicide attempt. The doctor ordered "rest," but rest and unpaid medical bills are incompatible. I was ordered not to write "anything of significance." Ten weeks later Emory Bergen, one of the few novelists I'd never publicly savaged, made me an offer I couldn't refuse.

He put it this way: "You need a place. I have a place I keep for contingencies—not much of a place, admittedly, but serviceable. I've been named a judge for this year's Wilson Walker Prize. They've doled me ninety books to read. But I'm working on a project that makes that quite impossible. Nevertheless, I don't want to step down from the panel. So, for the purposes of this contest, I ask that you simply become me. It should be a snap for you—right up your line. The board meets in four months. Out of the ninety books, you'll have ninety days to deliver to me your candidates for the top five. You don't need to write much: A page or two each will do. Just get me the top five and those I'll read. For the others, I need to know less about their strengths than why I shouldn't vie for them. I don't want to look like an idiot when the panel meets."

But I didn't feel like writing even "a page or two" on the book—the first of ninety—I'd read the day before. I felt the need for giving Emory Bergen's computer a quick online workout of a different sort.

The next day, December 16th—Beethoven's birthday, I always remembered—I wandered into Klinger's Café at roughly the same time as before. More or less the same number of customers again. I stuffed my gloves in my coat pockets and threw my coat onto the booth seat opposite Venus Magnum. The only change was that he and I had switched seats. I now faced the window, while he faced the serving counter.

"Wonderful!" he said, standing to shake hands. "Delighted." He immediately motioned to the young man behind the counter ("Rennie!"), stirring a finger in the air.

Within minutes Rennie (do names lend weight to people?) arrived with one coffee and one Buenos Aires Cappuccino Collegial—my original request from the day before. "You're lucky," Rennie told me. "They finally decided to loan us a cappuccino machine while the other's being restored."

I took a sip—hot, delicious—and commended him. (I also found it interesting that he'd said the machine was being "restored" rather than "repaired." I pictured an offstage heirloom in a room filled with Victorian clocks and Art Deco floor lamps.)

"It's Karma," he said, returning to the counter.

God works in mysterious ways, I supposed. But some things happen a little too conveniently.

I intended to query my booth-mate—Venus—on what game he was really up to. But I was momentarily brought up short. I found myself involuntarily staring at his left eye. It was, of course, displaced, as I'd noted before, actually set in his face wrong, nearly an inch, I'd wager, off-center. From my evening's Internet explorations I had discovered this was a possible indication of multiple facial clefts—but all unilateral: one side of the face only. I also considered but quickly dismissed the notion of Goldenhar Syndrome. Goldenhar patients show gross displacements of facial features, but in the images presented online, not only the position, but the aspect values—the dimensions—of the two eyes were affected. One eye might appear entirely normal, while the other seemed twisted in its orbit, raising or lowering an eyelid, leaving the eyes not merely displaced, but different in size and shape. The eyes I saw today, as

yesterday, had been full, round, and engaged. This morning
I also noticed not only the residue of the corrected harelip
but the mildly twisted extension of his lips on the same side.
And the cheek bones—

And suddenly the man winked. He winked at me!

"Caught you," he said. He raised his cup as if offering
a toast. I felt trapped into reciprocating. "Don't worry—it's
common," he said, when we'd each taken a considered sip.
"Not at all unusual to want to explore—the unusual."

But this was placing me on the defensive.

"Yes, fine, I agree," I said. "But that doesn't dismiss—"

"Yes?"

"Look. I want to be civil about this. I want to know who
you are and what you're up to."

"Isn't it I who should ask who you are? At least I've
given you my name."

"A name like Venus? How likely is that? You've read
about me. I'm sure of it. Where's today's newspaper?"

But of course today he had only the comics.

"My only question is *where* have you read about me?
Have you read my novel?"

He smiled the same smile he'd shown so often the
day before—his teeth reclining inward upon the tongue.
"Please," he said, as if amicability was his chief concern.

"Why don't you just admit it?" I wasn't angry—though
certainly peeved.

"Please," he repeated. "The coffee is good. The room is
warm. The wilderness of the city is the great and frigid out-
of-doors. I have given you my name and you have shared
two coffees with me—Where is that cake? Rennie!" He
motioned to Rennie with the flat his hand, rather as if he
were portraying a plate.

"You have *not* given me your name," I responded.

"I have of course given you my name."

"I have never heard of a man named Venus."

"And I have never heard of a man who does not have a
name."

"You know my name."

"I assure you I know nothing about you at all, except that you claim to be a novelist. You did say that, correct?—Oh, thank you, Rennie," he said, as food arrived.

"I'm a well-known author. I am certain you know that."

"Yes. Very well. I accept what you say." The small curl of his lips again. The double exposure of his round eyes, one displaced.

I would not let him just dispense with the issue. "I have written a *well-received* novel," I said with due emphasis.

"Yes. Wonderful! Rennie!" Now he pointed at me. "He is a novelist!"

A patron at a neighboring table looked up from his paper, gave me a dismissive look, and returned to the world of two dimensions played out in print upon page.

"You are laughing at me. You want everyone in the room to laugh at me."

Now he frowned as if injured. "Please, *please* ..." He emitted a deep sigh.

"All I want is common courtesy," I said with complete candor.

"Yes! Precisely! Courtesy is everything! So I give in. You need not give me your name today."

"I need not give you my name today because you already know it, as I have already proven."

He insultingly raised a bushy eyebrow, a look he rapidly replaced with a feigned expression of utterly pastoral disposition. "Proof? Forgive me, but I too often fail to grasp subtle arguments ..."

"What is this innocent ... this impossibly innocent look you give me. Venus! A laughable name! You know that it is a play on Nevus. You are trying to convince me that you in fact *are* Nevus."

"But Venus is not a name applied exclusively to women or wisely applied even then. Women whose parents name them Venus may have been unbecomingly cursed by this mistaken effort at parental benevolence—for example, if such a child, named 'Venus,' does not ripen so beautifully. That is seldom tragic, of course. Her schoolmates may degrade her for putting on 'airs,' but a name is not an 'air.' A woman named Venus who does not grow to beauty should be thankful that the true nature of her friends and enemies is more frankly revealed. Someone who vilifies such an unfortunate for putting on 'airs' is not worthy of friendship in any case. And why should my name not be Venus? How do you know that my father was not a drunkard who merely stayed long enough to affix a name to a birth certificate and then leave—simply evaporate as if into another dimension? Perhaps the name was given to humiliate the unwanted mother. Or was I named Venus on the heels of a botched circumcision? Perhaps I was not tragically born as you see me now. Perhaps what you see today is merely the unfortunate byproduct of surgical interventions set in motion because I was born with improperly formed—confused, if you will—genitalia. Botched surgeries designed to make me look more male or female not just at the level of the crotch or the breast, but even to the landscape of the face. Surely you'd not insult me simply for wanting to fit in with the crowd—but ending up with this—*door prize*?"

He was scoring too many hits. We had made it into a game of touché and he was well ahead. If nothing else, I would be done in by political correctness.

I lowered my voice. "I concede that you could be named Venus. I concede that nearly anything is possible so far as the laws of nature permit it."

No demented smile this time—he appeared to be doing his best to be conciliatory.

"Nonetheless, I think your purpose is a cunning one that you have not declared. I think you want me to believe you are Nevus, who should be welcomed as though a part of me. Even your reference to a father who might mysteriously 'evaporate' is no doubt an allusion to a disappearance in arid lands—such as Phoenix."

He blinked. "I have made no reference to Phoenix—and would not denigrate even a desert wasteland I had never visited."

Clearly we were stalemated. What I needed was a breakout strategy. One that undeniably proved the honor of my position and caused the collapse of his own.

"I—as you know but will not admit—am Altus Nevus Grande, the author of *Exegesis of the Cyclops*, a *well-received* first novel, as well as the author of numerous critical treatises of North American and English literature and a surrogate juror for this year's Wilson Walker Prize in American Letters. Whereas you are posing as—you are the counterfeit—the surrogate—of a beloved member of my family who died at birth, his spirit retained nowhere now other than in the DNA of my own body."

"I am Venus Magnum, as I have always said."

"It is a deception designed to convince me you are not Venus Magnum but Nevus Grande, who does not exist except insofar as I have explained to you that I alone am his one true surrogate!"

Who was *shouting*? I realized now that someone, somewhere in the room, was shouting.

But I did not leap upon the neck of the odious creature across the table until he said quite baldly, "Please, cannot we act as common men, as decently as brothers?" I not only leaped—I ground him like the flattened cushion of the very bench he sat upon.

Only then, and not truly before, did I realize the extent of the deception—as the room's gang of hoodlums and vagabonds and miscreants collapsed upon me, felling me in place, covering my back like lice and vermin—a frenzied mass of collaborators from the start—with cries of "Police!" "No, a doctor!" "Get him a spoon to bite!"

Who was shouting? That is what I demanded to know of them! Sirens in white heat were shouting. Sirens set over roaming, scrambled, ambulatory letters shoveled backwards

ECNALUBMA against the veil of some undetectable mirror! I still had eighty-nine books to read! I was the surrogate of the immaculate writer who could not bring himself to look behind him, to even acknowledge the pack (far more than ninety strong!) snapping at his heels, at the very heels of the Logos!

Doors, unwelcome doors, opened (I saw!), a body lifted (I felt it!) through those unwelcome doors by unwelcome white uniforms—I had seen it all before!

Under the running sirens, under the sleeves of buildings echoing the beguiling wails of the Sirens of Odysseus, I realized at last the final proof of my assertion that Venus Magnum was a conman extraordinaire: When I had met him yesterday, he had been disfigured on the right side of his face, yet today, sitting on the opposite bench seat, no longer facing the window, his disfigurement had decamped to *the left*.

My brother? My *brother*?

Not in a mirror will my brother shine!

THE OLD ASSASSIN

His name was Alden Brisket, but early on they called him Olden, and once he turned one hundred, Oldie. He didn't object. No one at Nobile Manors had quite seen anything like him before.

To begin with—when admitted at age eighty-seven—he had all his teeth, every one of them white, and not a cap among them. "Movie-star white, I call 'em—nearly lets me pass for seventy," he told Felicia, one of the elder-home's staff assistants who'd said something nice about them. "That and my tan and all this hair." His mixed gray-to-white hair was indeed wavy, long, and thick—neatly trimmed one-half inch below the collar. "Go on," he told Gloria, one of the younger attendants, an African American, "give it a tug if you suspect." His tan of course included a body-wide Diaspora of age spots, but age spots were difficult to sort from tan when a man was on the move, as Alden was every morning before breakfast when he took his run, out-of-doors, weather permitting. He ran a mile or two or three, always at a twelve-minute pace. A few times a month, he brought in a young female companion and locked his door. "Still got my prostate," he was fond of saying afterwards, well after the woman had gone, always adding an eyewink.

"He's pushing the envelope," Gwen Golden said, a woman of forty who'd been on the staff ten years and never known anyone else to have his way with the rules. "Martin knows," said Madeline Finch, sipping coffee while reading the night attendant's report. Madeline, though a tad younger, had two years more experience at Nobile Manors. "Laramie keeps him fully informed. If Martin cared to break Olden's armpits over it, he would have by now."

His apartment was on the second floor of Nobile Manor Four. Movers brought in his furniture and television, enough to outfit his two-bedroom, one and one-half bath, kitchen, dinette, and living room suite. He converted one bedroom to a study. It featured two walls of books and a large desk situated directly below a tall window he kept open whenever possible.

Alden's arrival had been both ordinary and not. Being eighty-seven was above average but not out-of-line with the clients accepted at Nobile Manor, which was after all not only a senior citizens home but also a geriatrics research center of growing repute. Above all, it was Alden's attitude toward life that set him apart from the ordinary. From day one, he'd predicted he'd live to 104, which meant the year 2050. "Girl told me so when I was fifteen. She was fifteen, I was fifteen. Maybe she thought we'd do it together. No telling about her now, of course. Named Betty Sue. Makes you blush to admit you ever knew a Betty Sue." He said 2050 sounded nice, that maybe by then man would finally have landed on Mars, that the world would start to get a grip on overpopulation—which was, he said, the primary force driving most earthly woes. This meant grasping the need for collective global action to provide fairness on a planetary scale to all conscious entities, including animals as animals were not—by any distinctly natural ethic; merely by the happenstance of power—a fiefdom of man. Not that he apologized for not going ahead and dying to make room for someone else. "I may be part of the problem," he admitted, "but I'm not suddenly going to volunteer as an advance guard for the solution." Not that either staff or residents listened long to such claptrap.

It was Dr. Martin Nobile's practice to personally greet the guests at Nobile Manor whenever possible. This wasn't difficult in the beginning when there were a mere sixteen units in a single manor house and geriatric research hadn't featured so prominently in the business. Dr. Laramie Nobile, Martin's son, was actually more congenial and the guests more receptive to him, though as time went by the prestige associated with meeting the founder was of course something everyone wanted to claim.

"The most *interesting* thing in my life?" Alden screwed up his face at Laramie, pondering. His eyebrows and cheeks pulled together, closing upon his nose as he did so. Laramie seemed an energetic and friendly man of roughly forty, someone you wanted to please. Alden worked earnestly pondering the question on this, Laramie's second drop-by visit. "How about the most surprising?" "Okay," Laramie responded, "I'll bite." "Good thing *it* didn't bite. Mountain rattler crawled into my truck once. This was in my photography phase. Left a door half open taking a shoot on a mountain bald in Appalachia. Tail *chkchkchk*ed right under my seat. I was driving switchbacks at the time. It could've licked the heels of my boots. I sure pulled over quick and scrammed." "How'd you get it out?" "Calmed down, got a good stick and acted very judicious. Flung it clear the hell across both lanes. Checked for comrades, too." "Learn anything from it?" "Yeah. A rattling reasonable story." They laughed. Alden only regretted they didn't have something worthwhile to drink. He'd correct that in the future. He found the younger man engaging. Maybe it helped that he didn't go around wearing clinical white, but dressed in a tie and sports jacket with elbow patches, a presentable but relaxed look.

In the late afternoon of a day Alden spent laboring at his laptop, Laramie dropped by as he now increasingly did, and stuck his head in the door. "Mind if I …?" "Be my guest," Alden replied, "I'm just making a note." He stroked a few final keys. "What'll it be this time—Jim Beam, or a good chardonnay?" The question drew a wry smile and a shake of the head from the doctor. "I'm sure you know the rules about alcohol." "Of course," replied Alden. "So the answer to my question is …?" The doctor sighed but said he could stand the bourbon. Alden would have preferred the wine, but kept his new friend company. Laramie was sitting heavy in his chair. He shifted as if searching out a zone of comfort he wasn't finding. "We lost Mary Graham today. She just didn't wake up this morning." "Yeah," said Alden, "heard about it. News spreads." "News spreads," echoed the doctor. He rolled the glass between his hands, taking a sip before adding, "As literally everyone says, 'Good thing to die in your sleep.'" Laramie repeated the phrase soundlessly, moving his lips. Did he look perplexed, or bitter? "Is it, do you think?" questioned the doctor. "You're asking me?" "Yeah, I am." Alden paused, setting his drink on a coaster on a side table. "Well, since I've never died, I claim ignorance." He stood, a thought in mind, crossed to a bureau, opened a drawer, and took out a small camera. "You mind? Just don't pay me any attention." Laramie wasn't paying him any attention. He had a distant look which he shifted to the glass cradled in his hands. Alden pressed the shutter. "We lost three people last week," Laramie said. "Now, that I hadn't heard." "This is in the whole complex, all seven Manor homes. I knew all three." "That's what we're here for, to die," observed Alden. Laramie appeared disgruntled. "Don't be funny, Alden, or I'll start calling you Olden as some residents do. I've told the staff not to, but as far as I know, they're likely the ones who started it." "Rolls right off my back. Don't give it a thought." The doctor stretched first his left leg, then his right. Alden noted the tasseled loafers. The staff wore plain walking shoes. "Well," Alden hypothesized, "if death is movement from consciousness to nothingness, then it's like sleep without dreams or sensation, so if you die asleep, sounds like no harm, no foul. Course, it's possible that you could find somebody dead in the morning who'd struggled for a whole night hour, fully conscious, but incapacitated, couldn't even push the alarm." "But we have a heart monitor chip in everyone at Manor House," the doctor responded. "Yeah, I know. I got mine." Alden had a small incision in his upper chest where the chip had been implanted. "But what's foolproof?" the doctor admitted. He tossed the last half ounce of bourbon down his throat, stretched his legs, stood, exhaled, and left. Alden studied his photo of Laramie, the man's eyes staring at the glass in his palms, his whole body slouched and sagging in the chair. Alden uploaded it to his laptop. He added a caption, "WHEN DEATH COMES AT MORNING."

What Alden had said was untrue. He did have an opinion on how he'd like to die, and it would be to die from a conscious state, not in pain or distress—sedated, likely— but able to register his last few moments of thought. Not that he saw logic to it. You could not take a final memory with you if it was to step into nonexistence. All you'd gain was a renewed appreciation for the gift of cognizance, just before it ended. It was a gift he thought he wanted anyway, the knowledge of alternatives. The random element in such a dream of death was fear, or remorse, or bitterness, or gratefulness for having lived at all. Who could guess what he'd think at the end?

Dr. Martin Nobile was one of *the* men in geriatrics. Baby Boomers, as they slid deeper into the 21st Century, wanted nothing so much as more of what they'd experienced in their first fifty years of life. Martin Nobile became the man with the reputation for helping that happen. The lifespan at Nobile Manors was almost eight years beyond the nation's average. It wasn't certain what he did—the guesses ranged from dietary supplements to randomized mini-bursts of exercise to tailored anti-oxidant therapies and varied biochemical treatments. Doubters claimed it was due merely to Nobile's selection techniques. Each candidate resident was rigorously examined; the doctor took only those *likely* to live long lives, screening out risks at the start—so the skeptics argued. Nobile had in fact documented all of his treatments as well as his selection procedures (aimed to establish rigorous baseline measures, he pointed out), and had at this point some sixty-four papers drafted for submission to *Nature, JAMA, The Journal of Geriatric Cardiology*, and the like, though the actual number he'd submitted for publication was small. He wanted a true longitudinal study, a convincing multi-year test—convincing to himself as well as to the rest of the scientific community—that what was going on at Nobile Manor produced verifiable, replicable results. He considered twenty years the minimum acceptable test period for reliable results. He was not a glory hound; he took his work soberly and demanded exacting measurements.

By the time Alden arrived, the first sixteen unit house had expanded to six more houses, each with thirty residential units. Martin Nobile did not meet Alden Brisket until the man had turned eighty-eight and the staff had indeed dubbed him Olden. Alden had gotten to know the man's son, Dr. Laramie Nobile, over numerous drop-in visits and liked the man. But with Dr. Martin Nobile, the experience was but a one-sitting formal interview to collect a life history for the record. The elder Dr. Nobile, thin and precise of movement, lacked his son's natural warmth; it started with his use of a video recorder and extended from there. The doctor appeared as if ready for public exhibition—an examination from the media, even—at any moment. He wore a pressed and possibly starched but open white lab coat. As he sat he fastidiously adjusted the knees of his trousers and ran a hand down the fabric of his red silk tie. Alden noted the gleam from the doctor's high forehead—his skin was scrubbed and polished to the pores. Every wisp of hair (yellow as warm sunlight catching a wall) was in place. His eyeglasses were of the latest style, perfect rectangles that seemed to hang in place with barely visible support. Like Alden's, his teeth were impeccably while. His nails were buffed and his shoes furiously shined. He sat erect, never slouching. He looked in shape. Yet, to Alden he seemed a robust-looking man with something dark locked within. Was he, as Alden saw him, in some way short of rosy health? It seemed a stiff contrast between this—wary?—man and his forty-three-year-old son, with whom Alden had played pool and poker and ping pong, the triple-P sports, they called it. (Alden was decent at pool and poker, but the limberness required for slamming wasn't quite there anymore in ping pong.) Could he picture any such personal engagement with this man?

Not to be wasted, it offered a mini-character study for Alden, who'd photographed many residents and staff—and plenty of public figures in his day. He kept his camera at the ready.

"Well, well," Dr. Nobile replied after listening as Alden repeated Betty Sue's prophesy. "So here you are at 88, and you're telling me we'll have you as a resident for another 16 years."

"That's about it," said Alden.

"Well, if you can do 104, why not 108 or 110?"

"It was foretold, and I feel it in my bones. I'm 88, but do I look it to you?"

Dr. Nobile paused. "I see a great many residents here, some who look older, some younger."

"That's not answering my question."

The doctor smiled. "I'm saying there's variation, and I'll not judge. I'm more interested in your prediction. Although I'm convinced the staff sees your conviction and may share it and I certainly hope to God you're right, it's possible you've underestimated your prowess. A prediction made all those years ago is neither a guarantee nor a binding limitation."

"No, I've got sixteen years to go, no more, no less, count on it." Alden suddenly double-thought. "Or are you thinking I'm going to make your program look like crap if I croak before I turn 104? That I should shut up and not advertise?" He snapped a photo at that instant.

The white-coated doctor sank back in Alden's comfortable chair—by happenstance, the chair his son Laramie took. *Was* there something special to this resident that warranted attention? "Why do you feel so certain? Why do you feel so influenced by a childhood prediction?"

"By definition, the older I get, the more evidence there is. Tell me, how old are you? Is there something in your experience that calls for doubt?"

"I'm just a data-gatherer. All scientists have to be."

"That's one question answered, and one not."

"Sixty-four. Feel better?"

"You'll have to make eighty just to see what happens to me. What if you're not here?"

"I have a son."

"And he can do the job as well as you?"

"Certainly."

"So retire, and take up a hobby. Or is work your hobby?"

The doctor shook his head. "I'm much more interested in hearing about you."

Laramie had long ago prodded Alden for his life story, which he was not reluctant to give—in bits and pieces—and which he expected had been passed to Laramie's father. Alden assumed that Martin Nobile was making up for letting nine months go without meeting the man the staff now dubbed "Olden." (Was it possible that Alden's doubts about the senior Nobile's spirit were in fact nothing more than a reflection of Alden's perceived neglect at not having been visited earlier? Had he in fact responded curtly to the doctor's questions? Maybe Martin Nobile was indeed a good but fatigued man doing that which motivated him to the exclusion of all else?)

Alden said, "I'm at the age where active life has ended, and the telling and retelling of stories has begun." He raised his camera. "Never mind this. It's just something I do." He snapped two photos, but stopped almost immediately, as the doctor, alerted now, posed.

A story was needed to lull the doctor. The requested life story?

"How many lies has your son told about me? He repeats what I say, I suppose, and who knows what fish stories I've told." Alden raised an eyebrow, but gained no response from the physician. "First, I was a bastard. Next, an orphan. And my first occupation was assassin. Laramie must have told you that. After assassin came inventor, photographer, journalist-astronaut, and the rest." Alden told how his mother's fiancé, a Marine, had lost his life in a freak supply depot accident—visiting an Army buddy in California, he'd backed into a moving fork lift—just as World War II ended. This was despite having survived landings at Guadalcanal and Saipan. Alden was born in February, 1946, an age when being a bastard mattered, in Georgetown, California, where his mother had boarded to be close to the Marine's family. By the time of the funeral, she'd begun to show. Though the family was supportive, Georgetown was a small community. Her sister lived in another small town in Missouri. The two, mother and newborn, traveled by bus. In Missouri, they shared a tiny room in his aunt's small house. His uncle ran a small but friendly and modestly successful hardware and supply store, earning enough to support his wife and their three children. Alden's mother found work as an assistant librarian, a job that didn't pay their upkeep. At home she was an ever-willing hand at dusting, laundry washing, table setting, dish cleaning, and other odds-and-ends. Thankfully, her sister's husband, a family man in an improving economy, was sympathetic. Their three children were eight, seven and five. The two youngest were now forced to double up. In high school, when Alden was fifteen, the girl named Betty Sue predicted that both of them, born in 1946, would live to be 104. 2050 sounded

like science-fiction, a dream that met the themes of the pulp
magazines Alden read: *If*, *Galaxy*, *Fantasy and Science Fiction*.
The next year two important things happened. One, Alden
attacked a school boy, George Jordan, who'd called him a
bastard. Alden tackled him, jammed a forearm against his
windpipe, and watched the boy turn purple. A teacher had
to pry Alden off his accuser. Two weeks into his three-week
suspension, Alden's mother was hit by a truck as she crossed
a street near the library. "That's when I became an orphan,"
he noted. "My parents weren't good at watching moving
vehicles." When Alden graduated high school, his uncle
gave him $250 cash; the best he could do, he apologized. In
the footsteps of his father, after ten months at a gas station,
Alden joined the Marines. He was nineteen. The first thing
the Marines taught him was to march on the run. It seemed
to him as though he often ran daylong, sunup to sundown.
The odd thing was that he liked it. Once he was trained, the
Marines introduced him to a hot, wet land called Vietnam.
From his parents' mistakes, he learned to look and watch: to
observe. On patrol, he became an invisible, silent force, all
eyes, ears, and nose. He spotted trip wires multiple times.
He learned to inspect before handling potentially bobby-
trapped objects. His fourth month in-country, an event
occurred that he seldom mentioned after the war. At point
on a patrol through thinning forest (the squad leader, Cpl.
Owen Flair, often set Brisket to scout), Alden approached
a large, open field. Here he spotted a uniformed North
Vietnamese Army soldier sitting and eating lunch not forty
yards away. The NVA's back was to him. Alden consulted
his corporal. The man eating his lunch appeared to be alone,
but there was a dip in the field in front of the man, where
other NVA might be hiding or out of sight in defilade. In
tall grass, it was possible. Cpl. Flair didn't think it wise to
shoot either a bullet or a grenade—it would stir any nearby
adversaries. However, he did make clear they wouldn't go
around the little rice eater—they would go through him.

When Alden asked about taking the man prisoner, it didn't seem to the corporal's liking. The corporal then backed away from Alden, adding nothing further. Alden found himself wishing he had a bow and a quiver full of arrows.

Alden told the doctor only the following: "Once I killed a man with a knife. It wasn't in me, but I did it." Nonetheless the words loosed in his mind unavoidable images. He'd had to snake-belly through twenty inch grass—grass he could today still feel brush his shoulders and cheeks; he could see the greenish-yellow tunnel of it ahead of him and above it the blue sky stretching over the man's head as he ate, the head behaving (it was a weird thought) like a cow chewing grass. Alden spent a full five minutes covering thirty-five yards. How clear had been the sensation that each minor *swish* of grass would give him away; that his quarry *had* to hear the movement of every green blade as clearly as grain being ground between stones to fine meal. With but a yard to go, the world switched silent. A single Vietnamese man in a North Vietnamese Army uniform sat cross-legged before him—not in the familiar squat of the Vietnamese peasants and commoners. His left hand held his rice bowl close to his mouth. His right hand wielded chopsticks. On his lap lay his AK-47. Alden couldn't see into the dip before the man, the minor bend in the landscape that curved down and out of sight, but he seemed alone. A single man, separated from his unit? A solider waiting for comrades to return? Chewing, the soldier studied the distant ground, tall grass ending in trees. Beneath the soldier's right eye a tiny mole sat at the edge of his eyelid. Now and again he blinked. No, Alden suddenly realized, this man, unknowingly, waits for *me*. He realized his own life now depended on a single act of concentrated, unrestrained will. He could not get it wrong. Rising halfway to a knee, Alden drove the seven-inch blade of his combat knife all the way through the thin neck, in below the right ear, out below the left; then Alden pushed the sharp edge swiftly forward, until the knife tore itself free of the throat. The man's last bite of rice, like minced fragments of brown spaghetti, fell through his gutted throat and onto the blooded ground. When the man's legs quaked, Alden fell upon him to crush out the tremors. His comrades—! (Were there?) Though Alden braced strong as steel, strong as the knife blade, resolute and set for the unexpected, he knew there were no comrades for this blundering, lone soldier.

None of this did he describe to the doctor, beyond, "It wasn't in me, but I did it." He looked embarrassed. "After that, they called me 'Assassin.' Can you believe? I was scared shitless. Never knew...." But he stopped speaking and snapped another photo. (Caption: PHYSICIAN HEARS ASSASSIN'S CONFESSION.) He never knew with certainty what had set him resolutely on a course to kill a man eating lunch, a man he repeatedly said he wished he'd never seen. Was it true? Why hadn't he at least questioned the corporal, or asked for specific orders? Was this action genuinely a necessary precaution against additional enemy?

In his year-plus in country, five men in his platoon returned in body bags, while eight more received Purple Hearts. Alden was thankful the corporal had not even bothered to draft a commendation for killing a man eating lunch. Much later Alden received a Bronze Star for more or less accidentally heaving a grenade in precisely the right place during a night attack, undoing the lives of three more men from this country he knew nothing about. (He received the medal because his captain witnessed his action.) He saw men die and he saw pregnant women—the first, the class of those no longer living, the second, of those carrying within them humans not yet born. "Only when I got out of the Marines in one piece," Alden said, "did I remember Betty Sue and my promised 104 years. So far, it was working. I'd learned to observe; yes, to put caution above recklessness. Even so, everything came down to luck. Could I get to 104 simply by luck?" Of course at age twenty-three, he wasn't taking the prediction seriously. But the seriousness of knowing he had but one life to live struck him like a bell. He planned not to waste it. His other lesson was his fondness for running: his never-ending love of the exquisitely set, efficient pace that he had gained in his first days of training.

"I got a job in a company that manufactured beach chairs. That's when I got my first idea: a beach chair with a built-in awning. All you had to do was pull a little handle and it flopped into place. No need for a beach umbrella. I named it Awn or Off. I was only an employee, so the company held the patent, but I got a twenty-five hundred dollar bonus, just about as much as I'd ever seen at one time. For a while, the chairs were popular. Sure, soon enough, others copied the idea, some improving it. The nature of business. I was twenty-four and eager. Next I invented a board game called *Profit and Loss* and sold it to Parker Brothers. It mimicked market processes, wholesale and retail and distribution and inventory, all that stuff. It only lasted a year or two—people had to *think* about making business decisions, and thinking involved work—but I made a little money and invested. This was in the early Seventies, with inflation and price controls. Not the best time for investing. By then I'd moved into photography, freelance at first, then for a newspaper. I wrote a few articles, too, local stuff. New businesses were being invented in garages. Apple, notably. Eventually, I bought a Mac and a tape recorder and I started calling computer people. The next thing you knew, I'd written a book called *The Cupertino Express*, named for the Silicon Valley town where Steve Jobs built his first Apple empire. The book did pretty well, at least for a first-time author. I got seventy thousand out of it, no advance, all royalties. At thirty-eight I finally started wife-shopping. I fell for a beautiful girl named Edin, tall, svelte, and athletic to boot, twelve years my junior, by happenstance from a moneyed family. Her father jokingly called me 'ruthless' and at times 'assassin,' so I wondered if someone had primed him. Maybe he expected me to take the opposition by the throat, like tackling George Jordan in the schoolyard. Edin and I were married that year. She put me through school. Graduated with a B.A. from Fordham in three years. A little pricier than VA benefits. Continued both the photography and the writing, and wonder of wonders, worked for National G for seven years, scribbling *and* taking pictures. Traveled. It was great. Occasionally Edin tagged along until we had James, our first. Then she turned homebody. When we had Toby, she said I was spending more time in Africa or Eastern Europe than with her. I quit and moved back. I still loved Edin, but frankly, as time passed, the love turned more into respect ... A common story you've no doubt heard too many times. When we had James, Edin's dad bought us a house to raise kids. Then out of the blue I got a call from the captain in my old Marine outfit, only now he was a colonel. And yeah, I knew he'd heard about my taking on the NVA alone. He wanted to introduce me to some folks at NASA. That led to a book on space commerce—space travel for millionaires who could afford a shuttle flight or had begun signing up for suborbital flights on one of the newly vying commercial ventures—even before the first commercial flight ever made it into space. The book sold about as well as did *Cupertino*, but $80,000 didn't really cut it for two years' writing. Edin's family tried to rope me into politics. I wouldn't budge, didn't want the money-begging that went with the job, didn't like D.C. much either. Hot and muggy as 'Nam. But we moved anyway. Ended up ghosting speeches for a Senator. Then ghostwriting op-ed articles for scientists, believe it or not. Actually, I was working for lobbyists who wanted to get scientists to speak out for this or that energy market, say. I could knock off a seven hundred word story pretty easy on nuclear safety or whatever, but, naturally, when you're ghosting, it's not *you*. We had savings. I told Edin I wanted a year to write a novel. She asked if I had an idea for a novel I thought would sell. I said 'Definitely,' so she said, 'Definitely, go for it.' But I'd lied. I had no idea at all. At the end of a year

I had two hundred tone-deaf pages I wouldn't let anyone see, not even my agent. Twelve months became sixteen. Edin figured out my computer password and read my opus. She said things like, 'This is serious, Alden; we've got to live.' But not with me, I guess, not after five more months of unproductive key clacking. I was fifty-two when we split up. The kids managed well enough, but I didn't see them, because frankly it hurt too much. Edin married a great guy who ended up appointed to a judgeship for the Fifth Circuit of the U.S. Court of Appeals. New Orleans cocktail parties, music, the harried life of the rich and famous. On the heels of that came my own big adventure. Another phone call from my Marine friend—now a general—and I ended up flying to the International Space Station as a journalist on one of the last STS missions. That was where my notions on the circularity of time came from. Orbit after orbit, Earth shuttling beneath us, day becoming night becoming day. Daylight bright beneath us; blue, white, inconstant and unpredictable cloud streams, then we'd pass the terminator, and soundlessly night took over, the dark below punctured by stars of its own, bright cities, meager cities, you could have scaled them by magnitudes, like stars in the heavens. Forward lay sunrise; aft, sunset. Always one turning to the other till if you thought about what lay behind you as well as what was still to come, time went both forward and back. You felt like if you changed directions, time would reverse. And as we repeatedly crossed from country to country, lands turned to cultures. Time and place mixed. All the ancient Egyptians were dead, but the modern were still living … and how much had their lives—or any of our lives—changed? Could you indeed just turn your head around, look backwards, and still see the ancients? As we made a single orbit, how many people had died or been born beneath us? I checked the Internet. Something like 22,000 births and half that many deaths each time we circled the planet. When I noticed dust particles or this or that object moving about outside the ISS windows, after a while I wondered how small an alien spacecraft could actually be. Those were some of the crazy notions I packed into the book. I sure as hell thought *I Was an Astronaut* would sell, but it just never took off. Then we re-titled it *StarGuest* and issued it in paperback, and it worked. Came out when other authors were writing anti-religion diatribes. Wasn't my intention, but maybe it fit the times. When was the last time you saw an America that so much as contemplated anything speculative or half-assed-philosophical? It wasn't till my sixties that I got those two sci-fi novels written. When they made *Golden's Mind* with my time circularity notions into a movie, I suddenly had enough to retire. Wrote three more SF novels, each under a pseudonym, just to see if I could still stand on my own two feet. Each was introduced as a first novel by youngsters Dwayne Foley, Daniel Hightower, and John Brox, respectively. Then people started asking why no second novel from, say, John Brox; was this author or the other washed up or something? So I did a second novel for each and each sold and here I was high in greenbacks and all I could honestly say was I'd become a hack. I'd never wanted to be a hack, but I was turning these things out almost like Earle Stanley Garner dictated Perry Mason novels. It was ludicrous. Of course, that's when the stock market jittered so I didn't stay exactly rich, but comfortable?—yeah. After that, I just laid back and decided to get old. Been practicing a good while now—successfully, too." When Alden snapped another photo of the famous physician, it seemed to jog the doctor's senses. He issued a sudden set of apologies, mentioned another meeting, collapsed the video tripod, and was off.

Afterwards, when others wanted to hear Alden's life story, he was glad enough to tell it, in episodes, but always minus Vietnam, and never mentioning the word 'Assassin.'

Nothing gave Alden more pleasure that his daily run. The Manor's seven houses included a walking path, which provided two very slight hills, and several bends and twists through both a sculpted wooded section and open ground. But Alden preferred to run the sidewalks and bike paths of the nearby residential neighborhood. Jogging in running shorts made a display of his knobby, thin, varicose-veined legs. T-shirts highlighted arms brown with age spots and purple in places where he now suffered what appeared to be spontaneous bruises—things just seemed to happen that way since he'd turned 90. He became an area exhibit. He ran wearing a red Washington Nationals' ball cap, touching the bill with two fingers in a howdy-you-do to anyone he passed on the sidewalk. About half would nod, some of them smiling. He seldom got the same reaction from other runners, people in their twenties and thirties or forties, who often appeared unwilling even to acknowledge his presence. I'm not one of them, they think, Alden told himself. They only see an old nutcase *thinking* he's a runner. At 91, his pace dropped to thirteen-plus minutes, and he seldom ran more than a mile and a quarter. Once, he passed a house where a man of perhaps fifty was in the midst of his warm ups. A few minutes later, this same man—as well-outfitted as a jogger could be, Reebok-this and Swoosh-that—eased in and paced him for a while. "I see you all the time," the stranger said. "Name's Mike." Alden said, "Alden." "I think it's great that you're doing this. Bet you used to run marathons, right?" "Sixteen times," Alden responded. "Sixteen! Me, I've done two. Don't think I'll do another though; body can't hack it." "Shame," said Alden, adding, "You look fit enough." "Well, I don't think I'd even break five hours—I'd be ashamed. May I ask your best time?" "Three hours ten," Alden replied. He was proud of it. It was a question he liked to be asked. "I was thirty-eight," Alden remarked. "A good age." "Yeah, wish I was thirty-eight again, too." The two joggers continued along the sidewalk which later joined a running-and-biking path. "Listen," said Mike. "One thing. Like I said, I see you out here pretty regularly, mornings. I'm usually just at the coffee stage of things when you scoot by. Frankly, you keep me going. But I do wonder about kids these days. Gangs, I mean. Maybe not generally in our neighborhood, but gangs don't always stick to home. Like that 'HOODZ' gang in the news last week. With the viper-head insignia? So, I was wondering. About security. I don't see any pepper spray, or a good, hard stick." "You're telling me I should have a weapon." "Pardon, but at your age, don't you think you could be a target? Some hoodlum sneaking up behind?" They continued a distance further in silence. Alden played with the notion of asking what would prevent his hypothetical attacker from swiping and using his 'good, hard stick' to bludgeon him to a pulp. Instead, he merely said, "Well, always grateful for advice." "Sure," the other man said, not wanting to offend. "Think on it, Alden. I want to see you safe when I'm drinking my coffee." Mike returned to his normal pace, perhaps eight or nine minutes. He said "Bye" and Alden touched the bill of his cap. I think I'll call him Mace, Alden thought. I'll say Hi, Mace, if I see him again. He'll think I've confused the name 'Mike.'

Still at 91, he confessed to Laramie that Hester had quit her visits. The doctor was surprised. "Wasn't she your steady?" Hester was a cheerful and good-looking woman of forty. "Have you given up sex?" "She said she thought I ought to. She was afraid she'd ..." Alden made a face. "She's concerned about my health." "Are you concerned?" "I like sex, but with Hester, we've been every other week for over two years now. Not that I can't afford it—hell, you know I pay—but I'm not sure I can face someone new. Not if they'd think ... the same ... which they're likely to." He stared at Laramie as if querying for a counterargument. The doctor, noncommittal, merely clapped Alden on the shoulder and left.

At 93, Alden gave up jogging. His pace had fallen to seventeen minutes, which for many agile people was walking. He began walking one of the Manor's treadmills. His pace steadily declined. He looked grim and determined but sour. He'd run for 74 years, and stopping was a big change. Part of his identity—the "I'm a runner" part—was gone. With sex gone, too, he feared asking the question, Am I a man? For the first time in his life he wondered whether it helped to remember the deep past when he'd been an Assassin.

On Alden's ninety-sixth birthday, word came that Martin Nobile had passed away while on a vacation at his family home in Wyoming. He was seventy-three, well short of the average attained at Nobile Manor. By now his papers were being submitted to journals. Martin had waited his self-imposed twenty-years to provide reliability to the data collected, and Laramie was updating the papers one-by-one to incorporate new data. Few appeared online or in print until shortly after his death. JAMA was one of the first to publish one of his preliminary papers. The journal devoted a full-page homage to the man's life. Other journals followed suit, publishing the Nobile studies as soon as Laramie finalized them. Two new staff members, one a graduate student in epidemiology and the other a postdoctoral gerontologist, had been hired to assist in the editing process, to ensure the papers would be soundly prepped for the peer review to which all journal submissions were subjected.

When he turned 99, he fell, tripping as he walked up a carpeted stair. The only damage was a broken tooth, which he happily held up in his fingers to show onlookers he was all right. But he hadn't felt all right. Something's wrong, he said to himself. Why had he fallen? All he was doing was walking up stairs. He spent the next few days surreptitiously hiking up and down staircases in Manor Five, avoiding Manor Four neighbors and staff, not wanting witnesses. A week later show tunes from the 1940s and

1950s started marching in his head. He couldn't stop them, perhaps because he couldn't quite finish any of the songs. He'd get mentally halfway into a lyric, and then the words would die. "Somewhere, over the rainbow, skies are blue, da-de-da-de-de-da-da ...." One morning Doris Day's "Que Sera, Sera" magically replayed unfinished in his head until past lunch. The tunes ran relentlessly. Maybe it would have helped if he'd sung out loud, but he sang so poorly that he avoided singing even in the shower. The lyrics remaining incomplete, he was often at the mercy of melodies for an entire day. It interfered with talking, because he felt like someone speaking two different utterances simultaneously, a war between the poetry of lyrics and the prose of speech.

In the early evening hours, a group of four residents known as "The Greeters" traditionally arranged themselves around a settee positioned at the front entrance to Manor Four. The Greeters were an institution before Alden entered Nobile Manor. On any particular night the four sitters could come from among a dozen individuals who made up the stable of potential Greeters. Ostensibly, they were there to help visitors trying to find someone or needing directions to the library, the gym, the tool shop. Absent visitors, the Greeters chatted among themselves. Hal Lazenby shook his cane in a friendly way as he saw Alden turning wide in the hallway to avoid the group. "You, there, Olden! Come sit a spell." Hal turned briefly to Marybelle Abilene. "Don't Olden remind you of William Holden?" He didn't give her a chance to answer. "Marybelle here says you're the spitting image of William Holden. Now there was an actor! *The Bridge on the River Kwai, The Bridges at Toko Ri.* He could sure act out a noble death scene." In his twelve years at Nobile Manor Four, Alden must have turned down forty invitations to join the Greeters, always saying he was at work on a new novel. But this particular night, his head was spinning, and his legs didn't feel steady. He swayed a bit, rounding the hallway corner, and felt short of breath. Why not just sit a moment? It didn't mean he was joining these people. "Good, good, great! See, everyone, persistence wins out. Olden is actually going to join us." "Quiet down, Hal, or he'll be gone in two seconds," said Eileen Sharp. Olden sat one space removed from the group who otherwise sat hip-to-hip together on the settee. He laid his cane between his knees and massaged his temples. "Hang down your head, Tom Dooley" played relentlessly inside his skull "Olden, you're William Holden's spitting image, for sure," Hal again intoned. Now whistling began to penetrate the cloud of Alden's brain. The Colonel Bogey March from *The Bridge on the River Kwai*. *Too-too, too-too-too-TOO-TOO-TOO*! It was corrupting, because he knew absolutely no lyrics to it—or whether the song even had lyrics. It might whistle through his head for days! Hal Lazenby leaned forward (he was sitting two spaces to the right of Alden), and said, "So, Olden, what's this great new novel about?" Alden, still rubbing his temples, didn't respond. Hal repeated, "Well, how long before you'll finish, do you think?" Abruptly, Alden turned toward the man and began whistling. "Too-too, too-too-too-*TOO-TOO-TOO* …!" He whistled until his mouth was too dry to go on. The Greeters, silenced, looked mystified, miffed, hurt. Alden, in some minor plea for sympathy, pointed a finger at his head, said, "Headache," apologetically, and shuffled on.

That night he had a dream—a nightmare—he'd not had since his sixties. In the dream, he sits in grass eating a bowl of rice, quietly, alone. There is no rifle in his lap. Somehow he knows that in an instant his vision of this field, these trees, this sky, will abruptly end. As abruptly as a nighttime television program interrupted—ended—in an electrical storm (the rice-eater has seen television in Saigon). The pleasant taste of the rice will be taken away. Whatever he had been pondering as he sat down to eat, that too will end. Something is approaching from behind. On its belly.

He is too frightened to turn around, fearful that he will face the raised, broad head of a cobra ready to strike. Is this dream familiar? Something unstoppable, hunting him—an assassin who does not speak—has he always, even since childhood, carried such a dream?

Alden snorted awake, felt the sheets against his chin. No. It was just that old dream. It is always good to wake and be free from it, that dark fantasy banished. He will be afraid to return to sleep, but he will. With luck, in the morning he will not recall an instant of it.

Laramie dropped by the next day, rapping on the frame of Alden's half-open door. Alden, sitting in a chair, swung a friendly arm toward him, inviting him in. Before Laramie even took his seat, Alden said, "I know, it's the Greeters, they've spread the word that I'm batty." "How do you know *they* aren't batty?" "Doc, they are batty, but they've got a point about me. For two weeks solid, show tune lyrics have been rattling through my head. Can't seem to shake 'em. It's damned aggravating." "Maybe we need to rethink your medication." "But I'm taking so many, where do you begin?" "Is this the only repetitive sort of behavior you're engaged in, do you think?" "Repetitive behavior?" "Compulsions or obsessions. Do you suddenly find yourself worrying about neatness ... lining up all your pens on your desk, rechecking the refrigerator door to be sure you closed it, rechecking trash baskets to be sure they're emptied?" "None of that. I've just got these damn songs in my head." "Do you hear the voices of particular vocal artists attached to them?" Alden hesitated. "Doris Day, 'Que Sera, Sera.' 'How Much is that Doggie in the Window.' Other people with other songs." "Do you ever hear the same song sung by more than one artist?" "Doc, who else besides Elvis is going to sing 'I'm All Shook Up?'" "Do you have ringing in your ears?" "You mean, tinnitus?" "Exactly." "Who knows? I can't hear past the singing." "Is anyone singing to you now?" Alden sat still, cupping a hand behind each ear. "Actually, no, I don't think so." Laramie watched Alden as he sat dejected. "Is it always pop tunes? What about selections from Carmina Burana, or Beethoven's Ode to Joy?" "No. Maybe Christmas carols. Not sure, actually." Laramie started tapping his foot on the floor. Tap-tap-tap. Pause. Tap-tap. Pause. "I can't get the tune," Alden responded. "I can't follow your rhythm." The doctor tapped again, erratically. Alden, not finding a pattern, exclaimed his frustration. "Whoa! Wait!" he cried out. "Oh, hell," Laramie suddenly exclaimed, looking at his watch, "I'm late!" At which point he sprang to his feet, waved, and exited. Eighteen hours later, bit-by-bit, Alden's head emptied of show tunes. They'd been replaced by the image of a tasseled pair of loafers tapping a floor. After a day, the tassels changed to penny loafers, then to sandals, and finally no apparel images at all. I'm cured, Alden told himself. To prove it, he sang (mumbled aloud) the entire lyrics to "Mack the Knife." When he'd finished, the echo in his head was gone. Sometimes Shirley Bassey's "Goldfinger" lurked in the background, but that performance was so great he didn't mind an occasional encore.

When he hit one hundred, they gave him his Centenarian Party. All the residents in Manor Four came, along with Laramie Nobile. They presented him a cake alight with a full one hundred candles. The number of candles was designed strictly for Alden, the long-time runner, the man with lungpower. So he made his wish and blew, getting maybe sixty candles on the first blow. Sixty looked pretty good to the crowd, but not to Alden. All around him people were cheering him on, "Oldie, Oldie, Oldie!" So he puffed again and extinguished another thirty. With his next try he killed the fire. He was glad. His chest was heaving. Laramie shook Alden's hand, and everyone cheered for "Oldie" to make a speech, but he was too winded except to command, "Let's eat the damn thing." They gave him the first piece, a corner piece heaped with icing, and he sat on a straight chair and drove a fork into it. Eating, he felt faint, as if his body had grown so light he was rising from the chair; no, rather the *seat* rose carrying him higher. But wasn't this familiar? As if … what? Oh. As if he were eating in a highchair.

A reporter asked him what had impressed him most over his lifetime, and he quickly responded, "The moon landing in 1969. And seventy years later, the Mars landing, only this time it wasn't an American."

He took up residence in the penthouse on Manor Four's fourth floor, the monstrous suite with four dormers. It was grand; well-lighted with natural light, the best suite in the Manor. Only centenarians could live there and only one. Alden just happened to be the only centenarian in Manor Four at the time. It would be his for life. And it didn't require a cent more in payment.

Laramie stopped in from time to time. At times Laramie grieved that his father hadn't lived to see the reception his scientific work had achieved. "It's ironic that the people he's written about—his patients—go on living and breathing, while my father …" "Lives through you. Everyone knows who's responsible at this point. You're memorializing your father, but it's your own work, too. I think you've grown since I came here thirteen years ago." "Naturally. I'm older. But don't think I'm contesting my father. I have no desire to work my whole life. I'm fifty-seven and I do think of retirement. Dad's papers are one thing. But the guests, their arrivals … and departures … it's wearing. With you, there's always been your prediction. But with others, the constant assessing drives me—damn near loony. I see someone, and now I wonder, how long … Oh, certainly some of them say they know when, but at the core they don't force me to speculate. I frankly hope you're wrong, that you're underestimating yourself. I'm concerned that you'll *will* yourself to die the day you turn 104. That your purpose will end. But I do think you'll make it." Laramie suddenly leaned forward in his chair, bent his head toward his feet, and grasped his ankles. Sweat appeared on his brow. "This job is like warfare. It's casualties, casualties, casualties." He sighed and straightened. "Well, if I retire by 60, you'll still be sitting here, waiting out your prophesy. And someone else will be in charge of Nobile Manor. Someone outside the Nobile family. I don't even know if that's bad. I'd better go before I put us both in the dumps."

A lden never mentioned his night dreams to Laramie. They came more regularly now. The recurrent music that had once played in his head was now replaced by periodic outcroppings of the dream: snake heads rustling like brush in the wind behind him; he was too horror-stricken to look. He'd wake hyperventilating. He was an old assassin, reliving his assassination. Perhaps the doctor could tap his foot and end the dreams? But Alden didn't admit them. An old assassin does not admit fear. Not this fear, which was of course inescapable.

L aramie kept his word and retired just before reaching sixty. He turned the research over to the staff noting he was available for consultation, but not to feel the need to consult him out of courtesy alone. He stopped by to have a word with Oldie—even Laramie was now beginning to think of the 103-year-old as a miracle who deserved a special name. "You're the constitution of this place," he told Alden on the doctor's last day. "What will you do?" Alden asked. "Write poetry. Try to, anyway. I did in college. Two were published." Alden was startled. "But that's exactly what I've been doing the last three years. Haven't shown anyone." "Might I ask?" Alden shrugged. "A long narrative poem. Titled 'The Assassin.'" Laramie looked weary. As soon as Laramie left the room, Alden realized he'd never live to see the other's poems in print.

Things changed during his 104th year, the year he turned 103. For two years, Alden had maneuvered about the dormer apartment using a motorized scooter designed for the semi-mobile. Now he found it harder and harder to mount or dismount the contraption. His crimped body now took a hook shape when he stood. His shoulders were hunched, his back humped, and he was rapidly losing hair. His hair loss had started not long after he'd turned one hundred, but had increased dramatically in the last two years. He now possessed a short white fringe around his skull—soon it would all go. His skin was changing, too, becoming almost transparent, as if instead of seeing wrinkles he could see his blood moving from arteries to capillaries to veins. He felt as if his skin was turning smooth ... smooth as peach fuzz. I'm going crazy, he told himself. When I started using those elevated toilet seats at 100, that was my mistake. Nearly impossible now to get up from a chair. Can't even take a car ride.

Now they fed him in bed. He'd wake, blink at the sunlight, think it was time to get into his jogging clothes, and then the eeriness of recent days would find and reorient him, bringing disgruntlement. Four more months, but there was no pleasure in looking forward to his prediction. The dreams that recurred during the night he acknowledged in his waking; they had become part of this now strange life. His birthday was February 14, Valentine's Day; right at the head of the Baby Boomer lineup, but happy days were not here again. He did look forward to seeing Laramie the day he turned 104, however. He hadn't seen the doctor in a year, and he missed their talks. Laramie, as far as he was concerned, was family. In the last weeks before his 104th birthday, he noted the number of specialists dropping by, pretending to examine him as if it were a matter of great importance, swabbing and even re-swabbing his cheeks for DNA samples, taking his fingerprints as if to verify who he was, exfoliating skin scrapings for some enterprising dermatologist. The week before his birthday, he asked one of the assistants, "Am I really bald now? Is it true I'm completely bald?" Two staff members held up mirrors, before and behind, to let him judge. The evening before his 104th birthday he grew alternately panicky at the thought of another dream and excited in his anticipation of seeing Laramie the following day. His vision blurred, his eyes misting, when he thought of the once young doctor, now 61. Soon he found himself talking to Laramie, so peacefully, it seemed incongruent with his actual excited state—it almost seemed a dream. Like the dream of the thing behind. So close in the peaceful grass.

The official time, someone reported to Laramie Nobile, was 12:01 a.m., February 14, 2050. "So he died in his sleep," the doctor remarked. He'd arrived at Manor Four at seven o'clock that morning. He knew from the birth certificate that Alden had been born at 5:01 a.m. and that it could be argued he was five hours short of 104. But deaths were reported to the day, not the hour. "I was so encouraged when I called yesterday and heard that he was still conscious, still alert. I can't believe he made it and I was late."

The obituary mentioned his former wife and his two children, now deceased. It also mentioned his books and the film made of one and the fact that he had jogged until he was 93, and retained most of his hair until he was 100.

Only later did the rumors start, rumors that seemed to have originated from the staff of Nobile Manor itself.

Sometimes the Greeters stopped visitors and told stories, quite as if they were true. They in fact appeared on a mission to testify to—certify, even—the true life story of an exceptional man.

"Oh, it's just a fable," an irritated man told his wife after they sidestepped the Greeters at their settee. The couple had come to visit the man's mother, a third floor resident. He'd heard the reports before; he, not his wife, was the frequent visitor. "A fable through-and-through. A man predicting the date of his own death—at 104!—when he's just a teenager. Stories about his fingerprints—not the records of his fingerprints, but his actual *fingerprints*—on his *skin*— disappearing just before the end, as if his skin had turned to butter; stories about not being able to reliably check his DNA, one test after another producing indefinite or even contradictory results, as if he's person A one moment, B the next, as if he'd lost his identity and could be anyone. That DNA business is utter fantasy! The idea that he turns completely bald on the last day of his life, that his hairless head becomes utterly egg-shaped, that his skin was smooth as a baby's or—an eggshell. An egg! You can see the allegory. Makes a circle of life. Damn fable, Natalie!"

When the man and his wife had disappeared, one woman on the settee shifted her weight.

"Next time it's my turn," Jennifer told the other Greeters. "I've never once got to tell anyone about Oldie. Do you think that's fair? Next time it's my turn. Absolutely."

As for Laramie, he attempted to publish his Alden paper in *Science*. The peer review process did not go well. Even though he suppressed the DNA results (he couldn't include them without being considered a fool or a charlatan), somehow word got out. He took it as a lesson. He was retired, after all. Anything he had to say to the world about Alden would always be taken as anecdote. Still, sometimes he dreamed about the old man. Once, in a heated ping-pong match, Alden slammed the ball so hard, Laramie had to turn his head. It stung where it caught the fleshy part of his neck just below the right ear. It stung quite hard indeed.

BERMUDA GLASS

C ole couldn't take his eyes off her. The maitre-d wasn't at his station, and the woman—mid-thirties, tall, lean, and stunning even from where Cole sat— was obviously displeased. She made a remark to her escort, a taller man of perhaps fifty with a deep island-worked tan. The man scowled and looked at the empty pulpit as if the maitre-d might be hiding behind it. There he found a menu which he happily retreated to read next to a well-lit aquarium shaped like an old diver's helmet, harboring multihued fish orbiting lobes of brain coral. The woman, not so tame, pranced in her confines, turning on a heel, so *frisky* in a night-black gown that dropped front and back, displaying in turn throat, cleavage, shoulders, and back. Long, tautly muscled legs visibly traced their movement in a slit from hemline almost to hip. Rippling skin, wasn't that the great attractor? And her never idle eyes, which variously consumed the princely glow of the sunset, the deep cricket-field green of the carpet, the starched primness of the white-jacketed waiters, the blocky cork-like torso of the red-jacketed sommelier, the whole accompanied by the clink of cutlery amid the chatter of diners at their tables.

By happenstance, Cole's seat provided a direct line of sight (just left of June's ear) to new arrivals. He noticed immediately when at eight p.m. the couple stepped from the elevator into the Galleon, the resort's sixth-floor penthouse restaurant.

A harpooned olive poised before his parted lips, Cole studied the woman's escort. Fifty vs. Cole's fifty-six, he put it. The enemy sported a likely $250-plus island shirt, animated by familiar icons — palms, orange-haired damsels, etc. — worn loose over crisply pressed trousers, yet betrayed a minor paunch which —

"What? What?" June said, as if Cole had suddenly found fault in something.

"Mm? Mm?" She'd caught him. "I was merely wondering how politic it is for a maitre-d to bow to calls of nature." He chomped the olive.

Not seeing the waiting couple behind her, June advised, "You've let your mind wander again. Fantasia."

So she'd not caught him. Spying was a hard game to play sitting opposite your wife. Cole's eyes had been moving like a metronome, tock toward his fifty-year old wife June, tick — a minor spasm — given the younger woman. Or was he pawing at a stray eyelash? As soon as the maitre-d (who'd returned from wherever) guided the couple in Cole's direction Cole had begun mysteriously probing a possible eye injury. His raised right hand now shielded him against any apparent surplus attention (surely the woman hadn't detected his earlier gaze?) paid the newcomers — though they were indeed (!) being seated at the adjacent table. Cole turned from diddling his eyelashes to buttering a dinner roll.

As with June, the maitre-d gave the woman the favorable seat. At the Galleon's forever rose-adorned tables, patrons sat impaled by view: of the resort's long, terraced descent, bungalow to bungalow, down to Bailey's Bay where even now, in the blue-green waters of late evening, discerning eyes could detect the dark wooden hulks of sunken wrecks.

Thus, June came to be sitting next to the unknown woman and Cole next to the unknown man.

Sometime during the course of the dinner, Cole's fork—an accidental slip—quite literally sprang from his fingers, arching like a trench mortar toward the next table. (He was a chronic loser of utensils.) When both Cole and his neighbor bent to retrieve it, the two men butted heads. That was how the Simons—Cole and June—met the Antons—Elson and Octavia—at the Tangier Resort above Bailey's Bay, Bermuda.

"Oh, that's precisely why I need the support of Octavia," Elson later noted in what became a dinner discussion held mostly by the men. "She's never wrong in her judgments of men. Her post-business dinner and office-party analyses always tell me who really stands where on the issues that affect work. Who to watch out for and who to have fun with."

"Fun with?" Cole said.

"Two meanings: Enjoy a round of golf with *and* make business. *Or* rap his knuckles because he's a blackguard who merits it."

"Blackguard?" It seemed a strong term. But Elson, a fleck of steak hanging yet from his lips, didn't explain.

"Well, as retirees, no such carnivorous" (he felt daring to use the word) "business dinners for us. June takes care of me just fine. Be lost without her. Even now, retired. Our last full day in Bermuda is tomorrow. Bye-bye on Wednesday." Cole raised his eyes—peeked—as he pressed his napkin to his mouth. (See now her proud vines of silver earrings, her classically high cheek bones, her mahogany-dark eyes.)

"Retired?" Elson looked stumped. "You don't look near old enough."

"Fifty-six. Cutbacks, buyouts. I bit three months ago. We haven't looked back."

But Cole was silently working to match the couples up. Elson was tall, yes, but weren't those starter love handles beneath the shirt? His face, though it reflected strength, was meaty and thick, a species of bulldog handsome. At six feet, one-seventy, Cole was a confirmed fitness freak—still capable of running five miles in forty minutes. June's looks were frankly very much guided by her emotions. Catch her when her face was alive with ideas, at such times she might still be beautiful. No gray yet touched the auburn hair of which she was proud. She walked two miles daily with ankle weights in good weather, played badminton in summer, and was a killer at ping-pong. She'd even taken up tai chi, which she said channeled her kinesthetic sensibilities. All because two years ago he'd asked if exercise wasn't sensible at this point in their lives—not mentioning her overripe hips, the tattooed network of cellulite riding the back of her thighs. And wasn't there a rosier tone to her skin, a reshaping of her legs, incipient and seminal, but holding promise if she stuck to it? Wasn't she happier for it?

Sipping his wine again, Cole aimed a courteous, perfunctory smile at Octavia—an innocuous smile, a pacific, respectful acknowledgement of her presence. But within those dark-caldron eyes, Cole believed, resided a maelstrom of attentions incorporating everything around her—the overhead fans whose blades shaped like dragonfly wings beat the air, the braying laugh of a woman too wide for her chair, even conceivably his own impromptu, nonchalant glance. Oh, she scooped it all up. Years ago Cole concluded that knowingly beautiful women held a plane of knowledge—of beauty's powers and effects—that other women never rightly fathomed. Unaffectedly, he stroked the back of June's hand with a finger, a public act of loving attention.

"Well," Cole pronounced at the end of dinner, "I hope you enjoy the remainder of the week. This has been unexpected."

"Oh, no," Elson corrected. "Afraid I gave it to you wrong. We seem to be in the same boat. Wednesday's it for us, too."

"Ah," mused Cole, "and here I thought I could give pointers. Such as the resort's water caverns. A nice hideaway—assuming you're game for a cold water swim. I suppose you've tried it."

"One of us has," said Elson. "Not me, I'm afraid."

"Well," said Cole, shaking hands with Elson and nodding to Octavia, the cold water swimmer. "We've enjoyed it."

After dinner, June said she wanted to walk the grounds a bit. She wanted to savor their next-to-last night on the island. At ten, a rising moon helped them see as they strolled. They approached a colony of well-cushioned lawn chairs where they could talk or not talk. But Cole, running a hand over the cushions, shook his head. "Wet." Spotting something in the grass, he bent to retrieve two empty wine glasses. June found another. Cole marched these potentially dark-evening dangers to a patio table. Clouds passed over the moon, cleared, and reclaimed it, an unending game.

"Maybe we'll take a wine-tasting class," he said, rejoining June. "Come on." He put an arm around her as they walked. In the fragile moonlight, the cement walkway that navigated the grounds spun gray ahead of them—a ghostly ribbon coursing in varied directions until it faded into night's landscape.

June was spinning ideas about tomorrow. They'd not yet been to the marine museum. And mightn't it be nice to watch one of the cricket matches they'd seen in progress on green lawns they'd passed on taxi rides into Hamilton. Her face filled with the brightness of plans. She leaned against him, placing a hand to his chest.

By now they'd followed the walkway past the bungalows and were just arriving at the level of the pool—closed since nine p.m.—when June abruptly took her spill, her body smacking hard upon the concrete plane.

There was a momentary stillness before the percussive quake.

"Damn," she said. "Damn, damn, damn!" She emitted a low groan. "Ohhhh … shit!" The expletive was less emphatic than the moan.

So, her home-forged athleticism had not yet prevailed. In the same way he lost silverware, she took spills. He kneeled to minister.

She lay lengthwise on her left side. In hopeful compassion, Cole placed a hand on her upper right arm. She firmly shrugged the arm free of his touch.

Patience, not sympathy, was the key.

"Can you move?" he asked after an interval.

Small moans still came. He could see her incipient anger. "Just … give me … *time* ..." Each pause held something caustic.

"All the time in the world," he affirmed. His knees ached from kneeling, but he stayed as immobile as she. It was the indignity, after all.

"It was the damn step," she eventually said, exasperated. She'd missed it.

He could see the vague contours of movement setting in. Experimenting, she raised her head. He wanted to touch her, but she said, "I'll be *all right!*"

When she regained her feet, she limped about in mincing steps, still quite angry.

"It was the shadows! Look. It looks like the step's not there at all!"

He had to agree. The steps above seemed clearly lit, whereas the last step was perfectly dark. Looking up, he noticed a spent bulb. "The light," he said. "You were a victim of the light."

But he knew that at that precise instant she had no way of thinking him but a fool, as the problem had been not one of light, but of darkness.

After putting June to bed, Cole found himself too restless for sleep. Imaginings and reveries—Fantasia, June called his ideations—camped for inspection. Driven by the stuff of daydreams, he suddenly craved perspective. He needed to be alone. Then he remembered the tiny observation deck just off the entry to the Galleon.

At eleven, he trooped back to the main house and rode the glass elevator to the penthouse. Ascending, he watched the landscape recede as the moon's illumination worked upon the small crescent of sand that was the beach, the bay's dark waters, and the ghostly roadway that connected the island to the airport. Had the moonlight only been stronger … It was not per se his wife's nature to have falls; rather it was her fate. She was no quitter. In the end, resilience always resealed their bond—when her mind spun with bright activity, when she stood and did not fall, when luck rode at her side.

The elevator opened to the Galleon. To his right a narrow hallway led to the Canopy Observation Room. It was a tiny, unlighted space, usually unoccupied; though in a crush, it held five. Wrapped in strong glass that yet shook when the wind commanded, the platform so absorbed Cole that he didn't notice a second presence until she moved. Mrs. Octavia Anton, in her gown with its drops and slits, smoking a cigarette.

"Oh!" he blurted, as if the wind were knocked from him. "Where's Elson?"

"As in, where's June?"

Was she grinning? Was that an odd, cunning smile? She stamped out her cigarette, exhaling in the small space between them.

"Elson's elsewhere. As you can see." She leaned against the rail surrounding the enclosure, propping herself on her elbows.

As if disclosing a secret, she said, "I know you, Mr. Simon."

"Please, call me …" he started to say, as she strangely raised her left leg, freed of the gown's slit, and straightened it as in a game of toe pointing. She rested her heel on the brass railing, rather like a ballerina in an exercise position.

" … C-Cole," he finished. He was unnerved, and he knew she knew it.

"Oh, I know you," she repeated.

He tried to visualize June and not Octavia, but there was nothing to peer into except the earthy smile of this woman's eyes.

"You'd just die for this." She aimed the toe of her shoe straight at him.

Cole raised a hand to shield his eyes, as he had when the maitre-d had sat the Antons next to their table. He protested, "I thought I was alone. I just came up for the view"—and instantly regretted the remark. Desperately wanting to look elsewhere, he could see the glass capsule of the elevator climbing back to the penthouse.

"I'll bet you'd really like to get in there and just *gnaw*." She shimmied her foot on the rail, her leg fully free of the gown. "How *is* the view?"

Bolting, he brushed past two men in their twenties who entered as he left. Had they heard? Had they seen her ballet?

Without his even punching a button, the elevator took him all the way down.

In the morning, dressed in swim trunks, Reeboks, and an eggshell blue Swizzle Inn T-shirt, Cole forged up the hill to the gift shop-snack bar at the main building where he collected muffins, one lemon poppy seed and one blueberry, both large. The strange meeting with Octavia now seemed imaginary cargo—mental baggage he could toss as long as he avoided the woman this last full day on Bermuda.

When he returned to the room June still hadn't stirred. Cautiously, not wanting to wake her—if startled she was prone to lashing out—he gingerly raised the covers. Her left ankle was badly swollen and somewhat purplish. "Not broken, I think," he said in a whisper, "just another unfortunate sprain." Was it always the left ankle, he wondered? She had missed that step at the Statue of Liberty. She'd wrenched an ankle at the very top of a Mayan pyramid. That time—at

Coba in Mexico—he'd had to run to make sure the tour bus, a quarter mile from the pyramids, didn't drive off without them. Had it always been her left ankle? Why couldn't he answer such a simple question?

He hooked a "Do Not Disturb Sign" to the door handle. Yesterday's heat, last night's wine, the tumble—no sense interrupting her tranquility. Through a sliding glass door that accessed a small ground level patio at the back, he stepped out and slid the door closed. The patio wasn't far from the pathway to the beach; he could come and go easily. Now that all the decision-making about the day's exploits had been cut away—there were to be no exploits—life became simpler. The patio held two beige plastic chairs. Here she could read her Nelson DeMille novel when she was up. Meanwhile, he read John Keegan, the inveterate warhorse.

But was he really concentrating on World War I? He felt some small, indefinable, nervous irritation. The last free morning was slipping away.

He slid the door open and poked his head in. Had he interrupted snoring? Now, she was a parade of silence. "Just to the beach," he said. "Not too long." True enough he supposed, closing the door. They'd been to the beach and been to the beach ... repeat history. Still, hot sand and warm water sounded a greater comfort than war history.

En route he hesitated at the fork leading to the small, but very nice, crystal caverns. Bypassing it, he mumbled, "It can't be helped, it can't be helped, it can't be helped." The third iteration was overheard by an older couple who now materialized as he approached the pool. He smiled good-naturedly, but they returned merely quizzical stares. Without a thought, he stepped off the last step onto the apron of concrete leading to the pool. Bathed in sunlight, it was the step that in darkness had caused so much trouble hours before.

He picked up a towel from the poolside stack, negotiated a final set of steps, and claimed a lounge chair on the sand.

The sun was fine. The clouds were pretty and conveniently dispersed. A better morning, he surmised. Off went shoes and shirt. Left and right he saw two small groups of children playing in the water, a father also. A half dozen sunbathers, too, but with the fine day, there would be more.

At a distance from shore, two women stood twenty feet apart in but waist deep water, an effect of the very gradual down-slope of the beach bottom. One woman was in her late twenties, the other perhaps twenty-five. Friends, possibly; who knew?

Might as well get wet. He waded in. This foot, that foot, one behind the other.

"What's this?" he heard one of the women say. Cole noticed the speaker's back and shoulders—her whole upper body, in fact—looked decidedly strong. A triangle between waist and shoulders.

"What?" said the other.

The first—the older one—pointed to the water near her feet.

The second moved closer to look. "Isn't that strange," she said, pensively.

Cole knew very well he hadn't intentionally headed in their direction, though now, as the water met his thighs, he found himself indisputably within their territorial zone. Without looking, he said, "A snakefish."

The first woman looked at him. He maneuvered to where he could see it. "Yes," he said, "snakefish. They're all over here."

Indeed, both women had strongly developed upper bodies.

"Well, is it a snake, or is it a fish?" One was trying to get a better look.

"Fish," Cole reported. "I had to ask the same thing. They look like coils of rope with a head at each end. And they just lay there on the bottom. Don't seem to swim about."

The younger woman said, "Thanks, I'm Sally. I'll watch my step." She had blond hair and a good tan. For that matter, they both had blond hair and good tans. Cole found an odd attractiveness in Sally's face, which was in fact marginally lopsided—tilted to one side. Flaws—freckles, weary-looking eyes, an oddly angled face—invited Cole's interest. Why? Were the imperfect more vulnerable? Might you expect a come-hither look from the needy? Or was it pure, counterintuitive aesthetics?

It turned out the women were Coast Guard rescue swimmers with two free days between assignments. Cole offered two-day suggestions, including his favored crystal water grotto. "Caverns mean cold water," said Sally. "Get enough cold water as it is."

A shopworn idea for a rescue swimmer, Cole concluded. He offered options. In the end, he noted nearby shipwrecks they could snorkel and for gear, pointed to a dive shack. "The wrecks are in the boating lanes, so watch traffic," he warned, retreating to the beach.

He settled back on his towel-protected lounge. The sun was yet climbing. Listening to small curls of water lap the beach, his mind drifted. Why couldn't June just trust him? The woman in the carpool had been five years ago. All else was speculation. Last night, he'd practically been a hero of resistance. In all their years, he could count on fewer than the fingers of one hand his actual transgressions. He was June's as long as she cared. If only she'd show more ingenuity: "Don't get resentful when I don't hop into freezing water in a cavern just because you consider it romantic." Waters Octavia had indulged …

Fantasia under the eye of the sun. How easily he visualized broad-backed women in wetsuits swimming storm-tossed seas to rescue imperiled recreational boaters.

Snatched in such Amazonian arms, would he feel only
safety, he wondered?

When he woke, the sun was high, nearing its zenith.
His watch said half-past noon. He collected his T-shirt and
shoes. On his way past the pool, he tossed his towel into the
hamper.

He skirted June's empty patio chair, slid the door open,
and stepped in.

Trying not to wake her, he quietly changed into slacks
and a polo shirt. He held his belt buckle carefully to prevent
a jangle as he looped the belt. He thought of making off
with June's untouched blueberry muffin, but didn't in case
she woke and wanted to eat in bed. Not a sound from her.
For the queerest instant, he almost wondered if she were
dead. A silly shiver of guilt. A foolish thing to think. All
her dumbbells and ankle-weights and speed-walking for
naught? It'd be uncanny if she could be whiffed out like a
candle, all because of a failed light bulb. Perfunctorily, he
stood over her. Without bending, he whispered her name,
watching her eyelids for a flutter. Her breathing was low
and regular, wasn't it? What had he imagined, that he could
have lain down beside her to take a nap and woken to find
her lifeless, cold, and stiff? Like a June moth to be mounted
under glass?

But the image of glass did provide a useful thought.
They'd promised not to buy each other gifts or souvenirs on
the trip, but surely June's accident nullified those rules.

It was nearing one o'clock. The choice between eating at
the poolside grill—where they'd eaten three times from
its dull, invariant menu—dispelled his sense of hunger.
He'd fast, make up for it at dinner.

He planned to visit the small glassmaking shop opposite
the hotel's gated entry. This would likely have been on their
list of the day's events had last night's moon been brighter, or

the bulb unspent, or they'd stopped to kiss just a step above. They'd visited glassmakers in Europe. Two days ago, they'd visited an upscale glass shop at Bermuda's Dockyards. But Cole judged their wares too stiffly accomplished, without the variations in workmanship that signified individuality.

As he walked, he passed the hotel's parking lot with its diminutive cars. Bermudans all drove small cars—even their vans were midgets. *Were* Americans SUV gluttons?

Before crossing the street, Cole reminded himself that the driving was all done on the wrong side. The hotel stood at the top of a hill where the road—often emphatically busy—fell out of sight in hairpins right and left, making it difficult to see approaching vehicles. But he safely skittered across, ending in front of the white-painted building across from the hotel.

"How's this going to work? What are we going to do? It can't be helped, it can't be helped, it can't be—" in a flush, Cole nodded at the two youths tucked into the shade of the bus stop, an unexpected social presence that made him pronounce the last word sotto voce: "—helped." What, precisely? A mystery.

Above the door to the small, whitewashed two-story building, the words BERMUDA GLASS loomed in large hand-painted letters. Stepping inside, he found a slumbering, two-room hot box. The entry-room featured two rather timidly oscillating fans, one wall-mounted, the other anchoring one end of a service counter. Two teens who were evidently salespersons—a good-looking boy, a better-looking girl—conversed alternately with the wandering few customers and with each other.

Here light penetrated, glinted, and traveled up, down, and across varied glass sculptures: sea anemones, starfish, dolphins, snails, turtles, sailboats, angels. The backroom was larger and included Christmas ornaments set in swirling colors. It also featured little glass men and women working at various occupations. Seemingly immobilized in the heat, a small, old woman in white sat in a white plastic chair blocking the glare from a back hallway. Behind the woman, long white plastic strips hung listlessly from the ceiling, marking a divide between showroom and whatever lay beyond—perhaps a stairway up? Through a skylight, the sun's white torch struck the white-dressed woman and the plastic strips, adding to the light reflected from the walls, from the merchandise, from the warm, weary exhalations of customers. Oddly, Cole's eyes momentarily strayed through a window to the exiting streak of an anxious-looking man with a beefy neck and head, a man in a hurry. Elson? Unlikely. He turned to the woman in white, who looked up quizzically before returning to her stupor.

Half-running to the front shop window, Cole gazed at the swiftly disappearing man. No, only an Elson look-alike. Weary illusion. He wiped his brow.

A snippet of conversation brought Cole back to reality.

He wanted to buy June a present, but in the heat, he couldn't center his attention until a customer in her thirties exclaimed to her female companion how much she wished "Alex" would buy her "one of those glass angels." Cole now felt the simplifying tug of gravity. Angels wouldn't have been his choice, but he liked fortuitous cues. Angels were found in both rooms. Those in the first room were the more elaborate: large and colorful—in penetrating India-ink blue, or rouge with amber halo. Those in the backroom were invariably smaller and white. None were flawless. The wings of the smaller angels were unfailingly asymmetrical. Either one wing outsized its companion, or the position of the wings differed, one a quarter-way into its stroke, the other a third. The clear-glass heads of the smaller angels were each marred by air bubbles. Though he liked the idea of humbled angels—heavenly creatures driven earthward by the errors of their (glassmaker) creators—the fact of flaws in both wing and face gave him pause. He fiddled with decision-making, sizing up the virtues of one object, then its brother or sister, feeling for weight, color, consistency. He struggled so with the angels that he backed down at one point, switching to snails, then sailboats. But the snails carried a question of balance: many felt unstable, apt to tip over when touched. And the sailboats tended to be over-sleek to the point of abstraction—forcing the viewer to guess whether it was a sailboat at all. In the end, he settled on the best balanced of the larger snails, and one of the small white angels with one malformed wing and a less intrusive air bubble in its head than displayed by its brethren. Plus a Christmas ornament. Ninety-two dollars—and over an hour's heated brainwork—for the lot.

Leaving the shop, he asked the young girl whether it was possible to buy a soda. "See the woman in back," she directed.

Famished, he circled back and paid the lady for a lemon-lime, or something close. She pointed at a back stairway, where he sat on the bottom step and drank. The blaze off the walls mocked a white-out. When finished, he crushed the can.

The heat in the shop had been impossible. Staggering—weaving—outside, while oddly adjusting, then re-buckling his belt (why?—was it loose?), he told himself to watch closely for traffic, looked to his left (the air seemed to dance with downy plumes lost from trees; tiny parachute twirlers twinkled in sunlight), and stepped immediately into something harshly oncoming from his right. A horn, strident; tires, a paroxysm of screech. A single dark, muddled moment. Had the brakes worked? Clouds cuddled in a blue Bermudan sky. How fanciful and odd they seemed. Kind words echoed amid the touch of hands. It can't be helped, he thought, brushing himself off. He swayed. He felt somehow turned inside out. Holding his bag of items in his right hand, and the top of his head with his left, Cole, embarrassed, distractedly bowed to the no doubt startled, head-shaking driver, before scrambling to safety across the second lane of traffic. In retrospect, in the glaze of passing time, he realized that even when he'd bowed apologetically to the driver, he'd seen no driver at all, because he'd been looking for the driver where he expected a driver would normally sit—on the left side of the car.

Facts whirled in his head. His "scramble" to safety hadn't been so effectively accomplished—he'd wrenched his right knee. He was hobbling.

What to do? His watch said 2:54 p.m. Nearly 3:00? He needed a drink. Rum this, rum that. What about June? He'd been gone all day, but now he needed time to recover. Was she still sleeping, or by now would she be buried in her book? He should have left a note.

Near the parking lot, he sat on a concrete bench and held the top of his now aching head, a pain complementing his knee. He checked his bag, its gifts. He unwrapped each. All were safe. But holding the angel, he asked himself how it could be 3:00 p.m. if he'd only spent an hour-plus in Bermuda Glass. That shop—you could have passed out from the heat. It validated any need for a nap. That backroom with its plastic-strip draperies leading to a cooler place, the place from which ghastly-looking Elson—or not-Elson—had fled (right?); that small upstairs room which the woman in the chair had mentioned, cooler with overhead fans. Into that little room with the tiniest glass figurine laborers forever at work, doing it, doing it, doing it, each one of them doing it, each *way* of doing it, the many ways of doing it over and over because it could never be done perfectly in just one try, not ever. Someone leading him—*she*? Upstairs? That scent and taste! *What had happened*? The dark woman in a place no bigger than the Canopy Room—the Octavian princess of light and heat and ludicrous confusion. *What*? That's what the thought was, precisely—*ludicrous*.

He lowered his hand from his head. It was red. Not bleeding badly, but bleeding. Had that car *hit* him? Had he really fallen? Had he been lying in the middle of the road, looking up at sky? Had someone asked if he wanted an ambulance? Had there really been a goddess in the glass house? Not her, surely. What would she be doing, lying in such a hot, confined room amid tiny glass sculptures? A flawless angel? And the distressed look of the Elson-man—that, too, was fogged illusion. How long had he been sprawled on the road? Had someone stolen an hour? Had he been helped to the roadside? What upstairs room? Suddenly he felt it. On the roof of his mouth ...and his tongue! He spat. He drew a finger across his tongue. A long, dark spiral of hair. He could feel others catching his throat. If he could disgorge ... But he couldn't. It was crazy! What did some stray hairs signify? He needed firm ground. He needed June.

He stood. He couldn't go back to his wife looking like this. Limping to the main house, he found a restroom off the lobby. In the mirror, he couldn't actually see the top of his head, but his hand touched blood. Not bad, though. He ran water, dabbed his crown with paper towels. He pulled up his pants leg. Skinned knee. Luckily, it hadn't bled through, but he toweled the scrape, too. The slacks were scratched, enough to require a new pair, but not an eyesore. He'd make do. He stuck out his tongue. Nothing. Thank God. He stepped into the lobby.

The hotel's first-floor lounge adjoined Jorge's, the restaurant for casual dining. The bar had dark wood paneling and a polished brass rail. One customer only, a late-thirties blonde, slim and gloriously tanned, sat skillfully positioned on the center stool, within range from either approach. Wishing to seem neither standoffish nor bold, he sat to her right, two seats—no, one, he decided—separating them. The bartender was a balding fellow about his own age, but with flinty-looking skin, tough, like hide. Cole asked for "something with rum in it." The bartender pointed to a card that showed the day's special was "Rum Surprise." He elected to be Surprised, and tipped two dollars.

He took a sip. Something sweetly brisk. Flexing citrus, a touch overripe.

"Ouch," he said. The bartender smiled, stepped from behind the bar, and disappeared down a corridor.

The woman was dressed in something silkily light, beach-lovingly colorful. Cole realized she was holding her cigarette for him to light.

"No matches," he said.

She pointed in front of him at a book of matches bearing the resort's name.

He pushed it to her.

She was despairingly good-looking.

"I'm not a second-hand smoke addict," he said. "Sorry."

"This can't be your attempt at subtlety," she said, picking up the matchbook. She lit her cigarette and smiled. "I tried one of those," she said. "Your 'ouch.'"

She meant his drink.

"Did it get your vote?"

"The verdict's not in yet."

Cole decided not to ask what might influence her decision.

"Actually," she said, "I know you."

Not a good sign: mental confusion crossing roadways, now faces too beautiful to be forgotten, yet forgotten just the same.

She blew a smoke ring. "Or, now I'm scaring you?"

He nodded, not to assent, but to politely confirm he was listening. Mentally, he was panicked to think she might be a forgotten former neighbor, an old colleague, a classmate … but certainly not a long lost girlfriend.

"I was sitting behind you on the flight in," she explained.

"Ah." He could forego the mental sigh for the physical one.

"The seat right behind."

"Short flight," he said. He felt runaway relief and a burgeoning sense of wellness—wrenched knee, banged head, or not. It was interesting to think she'd taken note of him—or had he and June had an argument she'd overheard? He didn't think so, as he didn't think they'd argue on a plane.

"That woman who kept talking to you and your wife— the one who said she was flying horses in for her property? She couldn't have been thirty-five. Can you imagine? Flying in horses to Bermuda from Virginia!"

"Yes. Interesting woman," he said. Relentlessly stunning, long-legged and …

"You bet," said his serendipitous companion. "Can you imagine spending three thousand dollars to transport a horse? I wish! And can you imagine what twenty acres on Bermuda costs?"

"Yes, we were intrigued, too."

At the very end, he reappraised the situation before ruling it out—he wouldn't be very functional with that knee, and he was already late returning to June. Plus this woman *knew* he was married.

He left wondering how impolite it had been not to light her cigarette.

After the Rum Surprise, he'd taken a circuitous route back to the patio. At poolside he ordered a Coke and sat at the bar. Behind him, guests in the hot tub gushed bubbly laughter. Cole considered an overheard phrase, either "lady in the grass house" or "lady in the glass house;" he couldn't tell. More guffaws.

After the Coke, he'd negotiated the minimum number of steps to their patio, in case June might see him hobbling.

He slid safely into the room. What time was it? *Five*? His head hurt. She was *still* sleeping. Now he had to seriously think. Was it possible that last night's fall had done more than turn an ankle? What was that red "ribbon" in her hair? Surely, not blood. Might she have hurt her head? A concussion? He'd better look. But as he approached from his side of the bed, he thought for a moment he would just climb in with her. Tired, so very tired, utterly and completely. Though he remembered to first hang his pants properly, and his shirt, too. Then he lay next to her, feeling immensely weary, and not a little woozy. He turned and stroked her mysteriously red-ribbon hair. She made small, pleasant sounds, right? Cooing, almost. He wasn't imagining, was he? Who doesn't love a head rub? Then he felt so smashed he simply had to lie back and be still.

In the morning, June found herself the first to rise. She hobbled, her ankle twisted and blue-black. She felt ravenous. She was surprised to see the muffin, given that Cole was still in bed. She sat in one of the room's two chairs and wolfed.

"You've been busy," she remarked, noting the bag on the dresser. She set her now mostly-eaten muffin aside and opened the bag. She found the Christmas ornament first. After that, the carefully wrapped angel. "When on earth did you buy this?" June examined it for some time. "It isn't what I'd have expected of you."

She set the angel down, and then noticed there was still something in the bag. She reached in, pawed the white tissue-paper wrapping.

"A snail?" She really didn't care for it, but she could forgive his strange notions of romance. Still, he hadn't said a word.

Okay, she'd take the first step. She hobbled back to the bed and kissed him on the forehead. His skin was clammy and cold. Blue. It felt like Jell-O stiffening. She put her ear near his mouth, near his nose. Why wasn't he breathing?

She continued touching, here and there. Cold, so cold he was … so like death. It didn't make sense. She'd fallen, not him.

Yet disbelieving, she called the desk clerk to summon an ambulance. And if there was a house doctor, please send him. She was calm, because this wasn't real. She turned the little snail over and over in her palm. He'd just retired. They were a team, right? Everything in tandem.

Then she noticed the small red splotches on each of their pillows. Like red rose kisses, she couldn't help but think. Like something perfect.

Weren't they?

DISPATCHED

And then he fell through the glass. That long night's maneuvers, the thinking, thinking until he was exhausted of thinking, and then that mad failed effort to finish before another hot summer day dawned—his constant carving away as if laying up provisions—all this had left him punch drunk. Though in the end, approaching mid-afternoon, it was nothing more than a dropped bar of soap and eyes too soapy to see that launched him through the shower's sliding glass door. To anyone who'd guess, it might look impossible for an ex-NFL lineman to slip on the proverbial bar of soap in a shower. But if the mind is black with confusion? He weighed three hundred fourteen pounds and having his mind sunk in a strange and unseasonable realm wasn't unreasonable given events. What did it matter if the shower glass *looked* thick enough to hold when it in reality it couldn't take the weight? All that blood, swirling down, warmly homing to a drain, as in that scene from the movie *Psycho*. Merely gazing from where he'd fallen, he could see the glass had knifed him in his shins, thighs, hips (and nearly his frontispiece), two or three ribs on his left side, his shoulder, and the side of his face. He felt blood from the top of his head, too. Worse by far than any after-game wounds in his eight-year football career. As in so much of his life, maybe it was simply another unknown rock, hurtling invisibly, a black rock cast through black outer space, heading for his little portion of the planet. He was in fact a bleeding hulk, only achingly able to arch his body over the jagged bottom of the door in order to snatch his pants off the toilet seat and grab the cellphone which, sitting atop his jeans, clattered to the floor, bounced off a heat unit, spun and scooted until it came to rest just within grasp. All of this on what should have been a fine Dixieland summer Saturday afternoon.

The 911 dispatcher who took the call was a twenty-nine year-old woman with thirty-eight months on the job. Jesse, the caller, spoke in a calm, clear voice interrupted by occasional gasps for air as blood seeped from a sliced lip into his throat. "I've fallen through my shower door. 1414 South 26th Street, Windom. I'm in the second floor bathroom, the master bedroom, right hand corner … repeat, second floor. Name's Jesse Stone. I'm bleeding like a stuck pig, though I don't see anything that looks arterial. I'm going to make it to the front door and unlock it. *Please* be sure the rescue squad knows the door will be open for them. I don't want them breaking it down." Dena, the dispatcher, a straight-thinking Southern woman, regarded the man as remarkably composed. She immediately dispatched the first responder, Medic 1, from the closest Windom fire station as she typed the address, victim's location in the house, nature of accident and reported medical condition into her computer, adding the caller's notice that the front door would be unlocked. The police dispatcher, a thirty-eight-year-old woman named Cheryl who worked alongside Dena, radioed the police, dispatching car 506. Dena asked the caller if he was alone and whether he could reach towels to staunch the bleeding. He asserted that indeed he was alone and that he'd grabbed all the towels he could already. She asked him to repeat his address, and she asked for landmarks. He gave two landmarks, said his house was the fourth on the right once the turn had been made. He repeated his plea not to break down the door—that he'd unlock it. She entered the landmark information into her computer, immediately updating police and emergency medical technicians (EMT) computers. She asked if he had a dog or a cat in the house, or any other pets. "Pets include snakes and pigs, Jesse," she said. He had no pets. He asked about an ETA. "Not long. I've got police and rescue on the way. Do you feel well awake, or sleepy?" "Police? I hadn't expected police." "It's standard procedure. They just want to be sure what happened." "Oh. Okay. I'm just trying to keep level-headed." Frig, what was he, a fool? Get your ass up. *Now.* "Have you had anything to drink?" "Ah … a beer an hour ago at lunch." He gasped a bit as he raised himself from the floor, his heart rate accelerating. She asked what he'd had for lunch. "Ham and cheese on a Kaiser," he said, still breathing hard as he stood and warily eyed the pools of blood. He tried to keep his feet free of the blood (before taking the shower, to avoid traipsing on prior footprints, he'd purposefully pulled the plastic sheet out from the bathroom—who knew he'd take this cockamamie dive through glass?), but finally had to wash his feet under the shower and grab a face cloth to clean the soles of his feet. He thought it'd be the logical act of a man trying to spare his floor coverings. "That's good bulk," the 911 operator told him, referring to the sandwich. He could have said he was a big man, but didn't. Yes, in the bathroom he faced the constant danger of stepping in blood or broken glass. He opened the bathroom door. All those yard-wide plastic sheets lying in an unending path across the floor. All that overkill, extra-precautionary plastic just lying about. Gang a-gly, wasn't that the saying? He knew he had scant time. "Why don't I hear sirens yet?" Dena repeated that it wouldn't be long. Then she ventured the unusual. "Forgive me, but do I know your name? Are you the football player?" "Ex," he said. "Retired. Injuries." And an agent not worth a damn. His mind wanted movement, progress, but it wasn't easy to coax his exhausted body to action. "Are you awake, Jesse?" Swaying, eyeing the chores that lay ahead, given the police, he said, "Yeah, I'm awake. I swear I'm by no means bored." Dena avoided a chuckle. "That's good, Jesse. A sense of humor." His tone changed. "Oh …" "What, Jesse?" "Nothing." He hadn't meant to speak out loud. He was urgently thinking what was where in the house. What besides the plastic sheets had to be dealt with … Shouldn't he get out of the house before they arrived? They could pick him up out front more quickly; that would be a medical boost, and maybe it would forestall entry. What the hell had he been thinking, just dialing 911? An arc of confusion had wrapped itself over his head like a bonnet, simply because for the first time in his life he needed emergency medical help? He shouldn't even have showered before finishing up, but what if he'd had to answer a doorbell looking as he did? "Are they still coming?" "Yes. They'll be there any minute." He was losing time. "Jesse, stay awake." This time she heard no response. "Jesse, are you awake?" She notified Medic 1 and asked how much longer. A minute later the first responder called. "Dispatch, Medic 1. We're on the scene. But the front door is locked, repeat locked. Given the reported injuries, we're waiting for 506 to secure the scene against a possible assailant. But frankly, there's no sign anyone's home. No car visible. How credible do you take this caller?" Dena didn't waver. "Medic 1, the caller sounded legit." She heard a low level consultation among the crew. "Okay, dispatch. I don't like to say it, but it looks like we're on 26th Road. You said Street, right?" "Medic 1, that's affirmative." "Okay, dispatch. Wrong address. We're not even near there. We're rerouting. On our way. ETA twelve minutes. …And we're supposed to get that newer, more up-to-date, nearly infallible GPS locator system in, what, four more months?" It was an exasperated, rhetorical question. The dispatcher switched her attention, checking for closer responders.

Within seconds, she realized there were none. Right at this instant, sirens, all those usually at her command, were on the run elsewhere. "Jesse?" She heard a low groan in reply. "Uh ...." He sounded barely cognizant. "They're on the way, Jesse. Hang on. It'll be a few minutes." When he did not answer, she notified the responder, again updating the computer. "I'm getting no response from the caller." Dena tried repeatedly to rouse the caller, whom she now regarded as possibly unconscious. More minutes passed. "Hey, guys. We need help here." "Dispatch, this is 506. We're here, but the door's locked. You did say North 26th Road, right? Wait. This is the fourth house on the right, but it's not 1414." "506, that's *South* 26th *Street*. You're on North 26th Road," answered Cheryl, the police dispatcher, eyeing Dena. "Look, our information is he's no longer responsive. Will someone get to the right place quick?" "Aw, hell," someone remarked. Another voice said, "Acknowledged." Dena was thinking how the newspapers would report this. Two lost teams—incredibly rescue *and* police—with invaluable time wasted. She didn't want to say anything blatant, as it was all recorded. Dena exhaled. Why *had* there been such a delay implementing the long-promised new city-wide GPS locator system? She pleaded, "Medic 1, can anybody tell me what's going on?" Apparently, no one could.

From time to time he heard sirens in the distance. On far off streets, seemingly more than one, but not his. Nothing ever seemed to work as expected, not 911 (thankfully, for the time being), football, or marriage. He had a ton of work to do and little time to do it. All those yards of plastic sheeting on the floors. Finally, he got to it.

All of it was Emily's fault. Fault one was that she'd been so bewitchingly beautiful. Three years younger than he; skin as smoothly tanned as if grown on Carolina beaches; a straight, honest, untouched nose (he'd met too many hygienically sculpted cheerleaders to doubt it); and furnished with an Ivy League degree, not that she'd (at first) shown any superiority about it. Only later did her eyes turn from enraptured green to jaded orbs. She was gone more than she was home. This last "retreat" of hers was not the thing for a thirty-two-year-old man with an active sex drive. Being forced out of football a year earlier, after a third knee operation, had not been the plan. But his life didn't end with football, nor should his personal esteem. But Emily had married him in his last active year of the game, without expecting this abrupt snuffing out of his career. Now they sat in a nice neighborhood with a formerly one million dollar home—okay, worth maybe seven-hundred now, but he still had the money to pay it off in fifteen years. Yes, a car dealership was now out the window (the auto industry cutbacks); but he was taking TV broadcasting courses; there was money in "color commentary" if he got picked up. So why hadn't Emily just waited while he sorted it all out? Could he really believe it was Sally Nevins (a thirty-five-year-old on her third husband, a sixty-year-old newspaper publisher—what did the man see in this artificial blonde with her surgically perfected breasts and her professionally acquired blaze of white teeth?) who had inspired these weeklong getaways? Ladies and gents dicing asparagus and sopping up soy milk with powdered pigeon? Purging? Replenishing with more soy and asparagus and pigeon? It would be Emily's third retreat in five months, and her second with Gavin. The difference this time was that Sally wouldn't be there; Sally had some ostensible conflict due to a charity function. So it would be Emily and Sally's brother Gavin Ross, "Mr. Muttonchops," as Jesse called the whiskery "glassblower artiste." *Gass*blower, he'd long ago decided, having more than once played captive audience to Gavin and Sally as they held forth with Emily in Jesse's and Emily's living room, discoursing about art; in particular, the plastic arts. Emily had been obviously won over; why else to start buying glass? That glass David and that glass Venus and that huge, ugly minotaur in the living room? The damn minotaur was oversexed and anyone who came in the house could see that at once. Mightn't his own friends (fewer of his old buddies stopped by of late, since the wedding more than a year ago, since the acquisition of new friends like Muttonchops), mightn't they get the idea that Jesse now regarded himself as nothing but a well-hung beast, and, worse, an advertiser of it? It could be hard to retain your balance in a shower thinking about Gavin Muttonchops artistically crafting about with your wife. ... And yes, what good had it done, constantly thinking on it, bemoaning it; when did it help to beg someone—your own wife—to change? It led to denials, to cries that you were paranoid, and to claims certain actions were justified because once you'd lost your career (and implied manhood?) you did little or nothing of interest. TV broadcasting? How likely? All of it cemented your weakness; demonstrated that you had no control of your love; that she was, in fact, no longer *your* love. It tested your ability to spell "cuckold."

W et and naked, he pulled his jeans on, judging himself lucky to have remained on his feet without stepping in and slipping on his own blood. He surveyed his sad shape. If he didn't get to a hospital nothing would stop the bleeding unless it somehow clotted of its own accord. How likely was that? He set the phone on the toilet tank, leaving it on, while working steadily. Quietly, opening a bathroom cabinet drawer using a clean washcloth, he extracted a pair of plastic gloves from a box of gloves and slipped them on. He then dropped the washcloth onto the bloody floor. Because there was a lot of plastic sheeting, he'd have to roll it as tightly as possible to avoid an oversized bundle. He'd have to roll it without standing over it, otherwise he'd bleed on it. It was chancy business at best, and he knew it. Once out of the bathroom, he closed the door, hopefully sealing off the 911 operator from any sounds of activity. Luckily, he still felt strong; no quavering weakness as yet.

To show he cared, he had to be careful about Emily's prized carpets.

Starting at the doorjamb between master bath and bedroom, swiftly but methodically rolling up the plastic as he went, he did a tight-wire walk just off the border of the carpet up to the walk-in closet. There he donned a windbreaker to stave off blood drops from the multiple cuts on his upper body. Had Emily been here, he realized, she could have cleaned him up, thrown him clothes, and whisked him off to the emergency room. But at the "retreat," guests were allowed (she'd informed him) one outgoing call a day; no incoming—although surely the retreat respected emergency calls. Not that he was going to call. Wait. He had to call, didn't he? Her stay at the retreat was supposed to end today. She wasn't home yet and it was afternoon. It'd be unnatural not to call. So, using the bedroom phone, he called and said it was an emergency and waited and bled on the floor while the staff at the retreat consulted. Then someone informed him Emily had already left the night before without checking out, even leaving her Blackberry and purse at the desk. He asked if people usually left a day early, and the woman said it was unusual, but unusual things did happen—except for leaving Blackberries and purses. Emily would have to return for them. He said "Of course," and was about to hang up when haphazardly, he asked about Gavin Ross. "They came in the same car and left in the same car. Your wife's. We've got his Blackberry, too. And of course both of their wallets, come to think of it." Surely, the woman was talking out of school, but now he'd been properly, publicly informed. "Um, wallets," he said. "Well, if she returns, please tell her to call me," he added before hanging up. "I've had an accident."

In his windbreaker and jeans (no belt and no underwear), rolling up the plastic before him, he dripped his way down the hall to the stairs, and down the stairs to the kitchen and living room divide. He continued rolling the plastic until it consumed the plastic on the kitchen floor. Now he leaned into the kitchen the short distance required to reach the cabinet that stored a box of black lawn-clipping bags. As he maneuvered, he caught two drops from his chin on the palm of his right glove, preventing blood from falling on the now unprotected kitchen floor. The gloves helpfully kept his blood off the lawn bag he snatched not to mention the cabinet knob. At a doorway on one side of the living room, the plastic descended in a long, wide strip down the basement stairs, where, after a short turn, it stopped near the deepfreeze. Most of the plastic downstairs he'd already disposed of last night. Now standing at the top of the steps, he rolled up the remaining plastic from the stairs, then wrapped it all in the large plastic lawn bag which he closed by pulling a drawstring. He then stuffed the bulging lawn bag up the chimney. Later, before disposing of the bag in the weekly lawn clipping recycling pickup, he'd add grass clippings to surround and camouflage the roll of plastic inside. (Or was that a good idea? Were county grass clippings used as mulch, and would some noble citizen or refuse worker report a blood-tainted roll of clear plastic mixed with grass clippings and tree limb cuttings? He had no idea. But he moved fast, otherwise any blood he left in front of the fireplace might look like he'd lingered there.)

Finally, he pulled off the gloves, leaving them inside out, and stuffed them into a jeans pocket.

Leaving, he closed the still locked front door behind him, keys in his pocket. He hoped the locked door would seem natural for anyone wanting to protect his property when driven to a hospital. He then sat on the grass before his front stoop. Sitting on the cement stoop centered by a crescent design in brick would have left an outline of his buttocks—a big buttocks stain—from his blood-splotched jeans. By now the 911 woman would surely think he'd lapsed unconscious, that he was drifting off, possibly dangerously close to death.

Maybe it would get the EMTs on the ball. Those guys took pride in saving lives, right?

Luckily his jeans held his keys, wallet, and butane lighter. He glanced about him at the neighboring houses. High hedges, high fences, and high walls prevented seeing much of one's neighbors. Who around here ever really observed anyone else, gave a damn about them? He burned one glove with the lighter, watched it blister, bubble, and dissolve into a pulp. Seeing the result, he lit the other. He dug two minor finger trenches in the lawn and stuffed the residue, one glove each, as best he could and brushed clear any appearance of divots.

How much did he hurt at this point? The cuts stung, absolutely, but so did his diced pride, his ruined marriage, his self-marred image. Not to mention this botched idea last night of rolling out yards and yards of plastic all over the house to catch any blood when all he needed to do was act like a character in any number of movies he'd seen (*Psycho*, once again) and simply wrap her *body* in plastic. Yeah, sure, nothing wrong with the extra plastic as a failsafe—if you weren't going to fall through your shower. He'd been yelled at by coaches for an occasional brain freeze, but that was a coach's way of motivating; on any given day, he was a bright guy. Just a little careless from time to time.

Once again he heard sirens. Distant, but louder. Maybe they'd be embarrassed at their lateness, and maybe he wouldn't mind smiling bravely at them in greeting. He was just Joe citizen, waiting to get crapped on, apparently. Though if wasted tax dollars had permitted this delay, had granted him the needed time, then there was some grace to wasted taxes. He tried to think of this as playing an NFL game hurt but stalwartly not letting it show. His ability to put up with pain and misery proved some weird virtue— didn't it?—given the EMTs' incompetence joined with Emily's despicability.

Maybe he *was* unknowingly bleeding to death, slowly, patiently, his windbreaker now all dark ruddy blotches and his pants consumed by voluminous stains. Surely it had been ten minutes, even fifteen.

A low burn consumed his insides. The 911 operator. Were they trained to lie to people? As a matter of policy, to reassure victims that everything was being done, though in fact nothing was being done? Lying to those in their death throes, even?

Blood fantasies. How easy to assume evil when all went wrong.

W*haa-woot! Whaa-woot!* Just like that.
Jesse turned at the short, pulsed, warning wail of the siren at the street bottom. It was a police squad car, very deliberately proceeding up the road.

The car pulled onto the edge of his lawn, the engine running. The police radio constantly squawked messages, call signs, codes. The officer on the passenger side, wearing dark sunglasses, eyed the bloodied man suspiciously. Slowly he opened the car door and stepped out, hiking his belt, his nightstick lightly striking his thigh as he moved.

Then all attention fell to a trailing siren. The rescue vehicle had arrived. Medical personnel were piling out on the run.

The police asked him if the front door was unlocked. He handed them the key, querying, "You need to go in?" "Yes, we need to go in." Now was not the time to act defensive. Instead, nobility poured forth: "Actually, I think I'm okay. I think most of the bleeding's stopped, though there's pools enough in the house. Emily's going to be upset over her carpeting. Her mom bought it as a housewarming gift." With grave earnestness: "My wife's due back any minute from a retreat with friends."

The rescue squad spirited Jesse away bandaged, with an IV and oxygen feed.

Had anyone listened to his soliloquy?

In Emergency, they closed seven major wounds with ninety-eight stitches.

At the hospital, still in the emergency room, not one member of the police asked him about blood spots on the basement steps or in the kitchen or in the fireplace. There must have been few or none—or nothing noticeable.

They did ask about his wife, who he said had been at a retreat, but had apparently checked out last evening, though she'd not arrived home yet; while waiting for the EMTs to show up, he'd specifically called the retreat to notify her of his accident. He explained about her friendship with Gavin and Gavin's sister. He said he didn't like it, and gave the questioner, detective sergeant Whitehaven, a hurt look. Still, he expected her home at any moment, he said.

Just outside emergency room J, where he'd been placed, there was a long consultation among the police, including detective Whitehaven and possibly a lieutenant.

Finally, detective Whitehaven presented his card and instructed him to call if he learned more about his wife's location. The doctors kept him overnight. In the morning, they sent him home by taxi, ordering bed rest, and special procedures for bathing until his wounds healed.

"Strange," he told the cabbie when the cab pulled into his driveway. "My wife's still not back yet. She's been on a retreat. Maybe I should have joined her."

That Sunday night, he noted on his laptop an email from Emily sent Friday night:

Jesse,
I've left. Don't try to find me or Gavin. From now on, we're desert people.
Em

When Jesse tried to file the missing persons information online that Monday, including a forwarded copy of Emily's message, the officer responding to calls on missing persons said Emily's note seemed to explain it. "She's not missing, she's gone," he said. Over the phone, Jesse heard a soft crunching sound as if the man were eating M&Ms.

"This email says so. But how do I know for sure?" Jesse asked that detective Whitehaven be informed, but the officer responded that Whitehaven was off that week, his summer vacation, though the information would be automatically routed to officer Strong, who reported to Whitehaven.

On Tuesday morning, the refuse company picked up the grass clippings as usual. Jesse had mowed the week before and late Monday night judiciously added clippings to the bag from the chimney and tossed this hidden bag with the two other bags. The refuse truck ferried the bags—three of the many thousands of such bags handled daily—to an enormous facility which dumped them within the horde of similar refuse. It was a very large operation, speedily servicing the needs of a habitually lawn-mowing public.

Not wanting to appear urgent, Jesse waited till mid-Tuesday before calling and hiring a next-day industrial cleaning team to scour everything on the first two floors of the house, working the walls and cabinets, bath grouting, furniture, carpets, and floors, anything that seemed worthy on the upper two floors. Earlier, on Monday in fact, Jesse had slowly and patiently worked the basement steps, floor, and laundry basin himself, not wanting it known that this area, which had nothing to do with his accident, had been cleaned, too. He stopped frequently throughout to ensure he hadn't reopened any wounds. He used his rest periods to continue thinking, planning.

The following Tuesday, detective Whitehaven, returned from vacation, brought him in. On the phone Jesse asked if this was about his wife—whether they'd found her. He'd called three times the week before asking whether there was news. "Did you find her?" He filled in the unexpected pause adding, "I want to know. If you guys can tell me what's going on, good."

For several minutes, Jesse sat in the small cinderblock room alone, surveying the cheap metal desk, the two metal chairs on the opposite side, and the two ceiling TV cameras mounted at the wall corners. More police observers, no doubt. Momentarily, he self-consciously placed a hand to his face, his stitches still present after more than a week. He'd declined a lawyer, didn't want sight of one. Had dealt with enough lawyers in football. After five minutes or so, detective Reginald Whitehaven entered the room, followed by officer David Strong. Seeing Whitehaven again refreshed Jesse's mind: a hefty, barrel-chested man of perhaps forty, his hair gone gray and long against his collar, and sporting a mustache Jesse would expect to see on a bush-pilot— something wild, maybe undercover-looking. Officer Strong, Jesse noted, was about Jesse's age, thin, possibly marked with a repaired harelip, and bearing a detectable glimmer in his eye as if anticipating an entertaining session. Detective Whitehaven said Hi, asked if he wanted coffee or a donut, and Jesse said he was fine. "We're recording this for the record, Jesse." He indicated the cameras. Whitehaven then announced the date and time, named the questioners and asked Jesse to give his name and address, which he did. He then asked Jesse to reaffirm that he didn't want a lawyer, which Jesse readily affirmed. It took a while before the questions began to take the appearance of a badminton contest, the bird pitched swiftly back-and-forth across the net. First, detective Whitehaven wanted to know why Jesse's wife's email had been forwarded to the police so late. His wife had sent the email on Friday; he hadn't reported it until Monday morning. Jesse thought it a weak question. "I didn't check my email till Sunday night. That's not unusual for me, not catching it Friday, since I don't always check my emails daily, and I really didn't get a chance till I got back Sunday from the hospital. Still, I noticed it so late on Sunday, I just emailed it to the police—and called the officer handling missing persons—Monday morning along with a request on the formalities of filing a missing persons report. You were on vacation, but I was assured it would be investigated." "We've checked. This," the detective said, holding a copy of Emily's email, "came from your wife's cellphone, not her Blackberry, which has GPS. Wouldn't she normally have used the Blackberry to make an email?" Jesse had already told them about his wife's and Gavin's stay at the retreat. Hadn't they checked it out thoroughly? Or was this a gaff due to Whitehaven's vacation? Jesse explained the circumstances at the retreat, the retreat's confiscation policies regarding communication devices, car keys, even purses and wallets. He added, "They had her Blackberry, but she must have kept her cellphone hidden in her car, which she could have accessed because she keeps spare car keys in a magnetic box underneath. Her cellphone can also email." "But it was a cellphone," Strong noted, speaking for the first time. He was doing his best to appear low key, but Jesse believed his tone belied a hungrier nature. "Wouldn't she more likely have called and spoken or left a voice mail?" "Well, detective, if you were planning to leave your husband for another man, would you want to have risked calling and having an honest discussion?" "You haven't gotten any further emails?" "No, nothing." Whitehaven took over again. "In fact, her cellphone's offline, according to the phone company. There's no chance, now, is there, that you yourself had possession of that cellphone, and that you used it to email yourself?" "Well, one, how'd I get possession of it, and, two, what if she had it password protected? Not that I know she did." "You didn't have possession of that phone? You didn't make that email, then just destroy the cellphone?" Jesse, behind his mask of stitches, made a hurt look, replying, "Really, now detective." Officer Strong stepped in again. "That's not all. There've been no credit card purchases made by either of them. What do you make of that?" Jesse smiled as if they'd asked a joke. "Well, they left their wallets at the retreat and never went back to pick them up. If you're like most people, you keep your credit cards in your wallet; at least I do. If neither of them kept spares or had other cards, like Em said, they must be desert nomads by now. Maybe they're living very frugally. Or on cash stockpiled somewhere, to keep them from being tracked by credit purchases. But really—I can't make anything of it. I'm hoping you guys find out." Whitehaven grimaced. "Look, we're not that far from *Florida*. No real desert's within hundreds of miles of here. Anyway, you think you could call your wife a 'desert' person? I've seen your house. I've seen Gavin Ross's house, too." "'Desert' could be a euphemism. My wife is obsessed with nature and health and spiritual wellness. She commonly takes retreats. I expect she has the desert in mind as another sort of retreat. If she gets bored, she'll come home. If she's run off with my dear friend Gavin, she won't. On the other hand, she once made a trip to Morocco, found it utterly and fascinatingly exotic. Now tell me that Morocco doesn't have deserts." Officer Strong smiled and turned to watch Whitehaven's rebuttal. Whitehaven calmly folded his hands in front of him on the table. "We've found both their passports, so they haven't left the country." Jesse smiled politely. "You folks must have done a bit of house-exploring while I was in the hospital." Detective Whitehaven then added, "We've located your wife's car, too." Jesse showed a startle, whether for real or an act being difficult to determine. "Why didn't you tell me?" "We've been trying to ascertain other things first." "Such as?" "You know that both your wife and Mr. Ross used your wife's car at the retreat?" Jesse knew this was ground they'd already been over. "Yep, the folks at the retreat told me. Could even be she sent the email from his house, then, if you found her car there." "But Gavin's car is parked there, too, right beside your wife's. Now how, please tell me, are they going to get from there to some 'desert' without driving? Or flying? Or to Morocco—if they left their passports? And without taking a taxi—we checked all the taxis for Friday night through Monday. No passenger names corresponding to theirs. And no pickup addresses matching Gavin Ross's or anywhere close." "Maybe they walked four miles to the mall. Do all taxi passengers give their real names?" Detective Whitehaven exchanged glances with officer Strong. Whitehaven said plainly, "I think you're being evasive, Mr. Stone." "Well, *does* everyone use their real name? You don't have to show an ID to get a taxi. What about buses? Or rail? Or friends who also like deserts? Maybe Gavin had desert-loving friends, people who liked escapes. Maybe they picked my wife and Gavin up at Gavin's, and they all drove off in merry fashion. But frankly, I'd expect it's your business to explain, not mine. You *do* believe I got these injuries the way I said, right?" Detective Whitehaven paused, took a breath. He scratched his head. "No one's disputing that. But let's backtrack a minute. There's something I want to get clear." Jesse shuffled his feet, stretching them out, moving his chair back. He cocked his left shoulder, then his right, trying to loosen up, though the stitches hurt. Whitehaven paused during these maneuvers, giving the man time. "It's just a few final questions," Whitehaven announced. "When we were originally at the scene—that is, as the ambulance was carrying you to the hospital—in checking the house—it's our duty, by the way, to ensure that no one else, a possible perpetrator who might have caused you harm, was present, or hadn't left evidence of his presence." "Fine, fine," Jesse said. He didn't know if it was a legal search, but he wasn't about to buy a lawyer yet. "In checking, we found your master bathroom door closed. When we opened it, one of our officers found your cellphone atop the toilet tank. The phone was still turned on." "Okay," said Jesse, waiting for the punch line. "You simply broke off your conversation with the 911 operator and left the cellphone in the bathroom.

To her, you sounded unresponsive, unconscious. In point of fact, you closed the bathroom door *in order that* she couldn't hear you." "No, I closed the bathroom door because that's my habit, to close all bathroom doors. If you checked, you'd have noted. There's three bathrooms in the house; you won't find a door open to one of them." "That's not all," Whitehaven proceeded, unperturbed. "Phone company records show that you placed your call to the retreat about the same time you stopped talking to the 911 operator." "Sure. I was leaving the house, when suddenly it dawned on me I should let my wife know about my accident. I didn't know she'd left the retreat until they told me when I made that call. And yes, I suppose I could have gone back for the cellphone to talk to the 911 lady, but then I'd have had to explain to her about my call to the retreat. And the bedroom phone was right there. I just wanted to make the call, and get out of the house and wait to be picked up." "If it had been me, I'd have preferred continued contact with 911, just to be sure about your rescue status." "Well, I may have thought of that after I left the house, detective, but I wasn't going back in just for that." Hearing that, officer Strong shook his head disbelievingly. Whitehaven interlocked his fingers, and leaned toward Jesse such that Jesse could smell the Juicy Fruit the detective had pitched before entering the room. "You own a firearm, Mr. Stone?" "I own a handgun, yes. I expect you know, since it's registered. And it hasn't been fired since I bought it five years ago when I first tested it on a range." "You know how far it is from Gavin Ross's house to yours?" "No." "Okay, I'll tell you. Eight miles. Can you run eight miles, Mr. Stone?" "How would I be at Gavin's in the first place?" "If you murdered your wife and Gavin at your house, then drove your wife's car back to his place. So again: Can you run eight miles, Mr. Stone?" Jesse smiled a comfortable smile, "My heart can, but not my knees. Call my doctor's office." The two officers didn't look pleased.

Jesse had known they didn't have anything on him when they didn't hold him at the hospital. Leaving the cellphone in the bathroom wasn't a crime. And he wasn't sure about the legality of checking his phone records without a warrant, but perhaps that could be considered part of a missing persons follow up. If the damn fools never opened the deepfreeze and at least poked two feet down, they had themselves to blame. If they believed that under conditions of absolute necessity he really couldn't run the eight miles from Ross's house back home after leaving his wife's car, and if they'd never even considered that he'd biked the thirty-seven miles to the retreat, pitching the cheap bike two miles off and walking the rest, carrying the handgun to force them into Emily's car to drive them both to his home where he went to work on them ... Secured hands, taped mouths, and wrapped blindfolds; the plastic bag slipped immediately over Gavin's head, then just as quickly taped shut—and when could an even death-panicked Gavin outdo the bear-grasp of a NFL lineman? Next, carrying his wife upstairs to the bedroom, not for a farewell kiss, but a true Hitchcock shower scene in the same shower they'd had such nice times on past occasions, more and more remotely past of late, however ... Afterwards, of course, he had to lay all that plastic sheeting (in addition to wrapping her body in plastic; he'd taken this double measure of care—yes, a bit foolish, in the end) before carrying her to the basement, where he'd gone to work on two still warm bodies, making temporary hiding places for all their parts ... If both of them—police *and* rescue squads drove to wrong addresses—why should he have ever worried anyone would get anything else right? Though it would have been easier if he had finished cleaning up the house before deciding to take a Saturday afternoon shower of his own, overlooking that little bar of soap.

Four weeks after placing his 911 call, Jesse called the business office number for 911—the number the public would use to reach 911 administrative offices without making a 911 call for an emergency. He explained who he was and said he wanted to thank the nice woman who'd worked his case. The man who answered said he'd take a message and pass it along.

Two hours later, Jesse received a call from a woman who identified herself as Dena.

"Dena?" Was it her?

"I was your 911 operator. You called me?"

"Oh, yeah." Jesse quickly swallowed some Fritos he was eating. "I wanted to thank you."

"You wanted to thank me? To be honest …" She sighed, a long sigh that sounded one of embarrassment.

Jesse was surprised how much he suddenly liked the woman's voice, despite his earlier conclusions. At this point, he felt he understood better how the best of systems (or plans) could have snafus, how so much could turn on luck, good or bad.

"Look," he said. "If you're feeling things didn't go as well as you'd like, but you can't say that because of some 911 management policy about compromising the public's image of system integrity, I respect that. But really, I do appreciate what you did for me. I know there must have been some frustration, but you hung in there and did what you were supposed to do. They put near a hundred stitches in me. In fact, parts of me got glued back together." (He thought that sounded good, true or not.) "So as far as I'm concerned, you're the one who saved my life."

"Well … I appreciate that," she said after a hesitation.

Did she sound remorseful? Timid? One thing she did sound … She sounded young; she *sounded* attractive. A fluid voice could lead to certain fluidly of visual imagery, Jesse believed. He was confident of it. He *believed* in this woman's attractiveness.

He took the next step. "I'm kind of alone these days. You may have heard about my wife … being gone with some guy. No one seems to know where." He waited, but she said nothing. He continued, "I haven't had dinner with anyone in a while. You sound nice."

He heard a slight intake of breath, but she said nothing.

"You working 911 tonight?"

"No, as a matter of fact."

"Well, how's the idea sound to you?"

"What idea, precisely?"

It was a great dinner. Lamb kabobs with rice and pita bread and two bottles of red wine. He saw the way her eyes moved about the table, centering on the utensils, the food, the waiters, and of course Jesse, too. She had a bright face and she smiled and blushed too, often at the slightest compliment he paid her. He had the oddest passion to tell her how Middle Easterners slaughtered lambs for feast days. How he'd seen it done once in Turkey. How they slit their throats and let the blood run. He wanted to tell her and end the story with some catchy, cosmopolitan remark, such as, "It was rather interesting, actually." But of course to the average person it was gruesome, too, and she'd think him weird, so he had no intention of mentioning it. He never tried telling it to her, but he wondered if it was a story he could tell when he graduated from broadcasting school and got a "color" job as an announcer with ESPN or one of the other media, when "the guys" met or had dinner together during their off hours.

He spent six months taking one by one the eighteen individually wrapped gray plastic bundles out from his by now numerous hiding places for a drive in the car, whenever he felt like exploring some new, offbeat, hopefully unfrequented place. In the fall and spring it was refreshing to let the top down on the Lexus he'd planned to buy for Em but ended up buying for himself—and just drive.

MRS. HARRIS ADMIRES
THE PERSEIDS

A week ahead, Jerome phoned and invited the widowed Mrs. Harris, Samantha Harris, for the two-hour afternoon drive on August 12th, specifically to view the Perseids, the annual meteor shower expected to peak that night.

Mrs. Harris's first response was a crinkled brow and a question. "What on earth for?" Generally, Mrs. Harris translated most male-female interactions to sex. That had certainly been her experience before marriage and later as she watched so many friends succumb to external temptations once married. Disclosures over lunch taught her to count affairs—at least one, very likely two, three, or four—as common. A considerable age gap also stood between her and Jerome. Mrs. Harris was forty-three, while Jerome was likely ten years younger. Not that Mrs. Harris hadn't retained her auburn hair, her hazel eyes, and her devastatingly persuasive figure. But it was also true that the two didn't really know each other. Yes, Jerome had worked six years as Mrs. Harris's late husband Harry's accountant in his building supply company and had served as a pallbearer at his funeral five months ago. Indeed, Jerome's longtime allegiance to Harry in itself seemed so strong she'd have speculated Jerome to be overpowered by internal feelings of disloyalty if he moved on her. If he really had making a "move" in mind. But what else did she know? Did he have hobbies (beyond, evidently, astronomy)? Was he athletic? Did he have a sense of humor? Was he bull-headed and argumentative or a paragon of reasonability? To add to the gap in age and acquaintance was another: physical attraction. Where Harry had been bulky and firm, Jerome was nondescript. He was average in every way she could think of. Throw him into any shopping mall and try picking him out. Height and build—the next guy's. Eyes, hair: brown. Hair always trimmed. (Weekly cuts?) A bland face, neither sallow and thin, nor pudgy and round, nor angular and long. Bland. No peaks, valleys, divots, creases, or lines. Yet, for all that, he *did* look pleasant. Even his strange phone call demonstrated the unexpected—a capability for optimism—or possible audacity? And yet, whenever she thought of Jerome (almost never), she irrevocably thought also of Harry. As if the two were locked-in-step, but now with the leader gone. Was he seeking a substitute friend?

So, when he had suggested the trip, she had responded, "What on earth for?"

"That's catchy, your phrase 'what on earth for?,'" Jerome replied, "because we're dealing with something that's really not of this earth."

Strangely, at that point, he hung up.

Mrs. Harris had been sitting in a rocker on the large gray-painted porch of her late Victorian house, peering both at her dead cellphone and at a patch of possibly corrupt thistle in her garden, just as Jerome, on foot, stopped in front. Evidently, he'd been thinking this out. Without a moment's hesitation, simply saying, "Hi," he opened the gate, crossed the walkway and mounted the porch. There was a second rocker, but Jerome, knowing it must have been Harry's, didn't sit.

"Once upon a time," he started his lecture, "there was a comet that passed this way, and afterwards, never reappeared. Instead once every year we run the gauntlet of the comet's residue, and that's the Perseid meteor shower. Every year it's either the Perseids or the Leonids—that one's in the winter—that turn out to be the gassers."

"'Gassers?'" Mrs. Harris replied.

"I just mean they put on the best show. I've got a cabin in West Virginia, not a long drive. There are good restaurants. The cabin's got a loft bedroom and a bedroom below. Kitchen, bath, all those things. Long deck on the front. Harry advised me on both planning and construction. I bought materials on discount, worked weekends and vacations, and three years later I had a finished cabin. Harry came out a couple times to check for things building inspectors wouldn't let pass. Overall, he seemed pleased, and I think you'd like it."

"I'm still not sure what you're asking," Mrs. Harris responded. "You're saying you want me to go to your cabin to watch—shooting stars? Overnight?"

"Yes. That's about it. Please remember, two bedrooms. I mentioned it to Harry last September asking both of you to come and he thought it might be nice. It's dark sky out there, not all lit up like around D.C., and you sit on the deck just like you're sitting on your porch right now. You train your eyes in the right direction, and the closer you get to midnight the more meteorites appear. After midnight, two a.m. or so, that's the best."

"Two a.m.?" Mrs. Harris stopped rocking. "Two in the morning?"

"Yeah. You don't have to stay up that late. You could always go to bed, but I'd recommend holding out for one a.m. anyway. Once these things get going, they can be magical. Better than the Fourth of July. Put's a sense of 'awe' back into things. Look, it's a week away, so you could think about it and I'll check back."

"What if the weather's bad?"

"Then we won't go."

"Harry really approved of this?"

Without comment, the accountant nodded his head.

Mrs. Harris seemed agitated. She began rocking faster, but eased as she scanned the reassuringly deeply cloud-covered skies. If weather was the key, it seemed unlikely that in a week conditions would change all that much.

"Harry never mentioned this to me."

"When I raised it, he said he'd never seen a meteor shower, but always wanted to. Maybe he wanted to surprise you. Look. I'll check back on the 11th. On the 12th, if the weather's good, I'll come by about two p.m., get a jump on rush hour, and we'll drive out and eat—there's a restaurant with a spectacular view of the mountains, sitting just above the valley with my cabin. Then we'd just sit on the deck, open some wine, and wait for the show. Then sleep, wake, and breakfast someplace. I'd have you back noon the next day."

"How many bathrooms does your place have?"

"Just one, but it's spacious."

Mrs. Harris again regarded the skies.

"Well, possibly," she said. She looked perturbed and uncertain, but Jerome heard her response as an affirmation.

That's the way it was left as he returned to his walk, waving once to Mrs. Harris, who did not acknowledge it.

For two days, Mrs. Harris watched the clouds darken. An even safer bet she'd never have to worry about taking the trip?

But wasn't that still the problem: Ignorance? Ignorance that might be quelled if she sleuthed and had some luck at it. So she began thumbing Harry's diary, something she'd never read. Oddly, she wasn't sure she wanted to discover all her husband's secret thoughts. He'd kept diaries the last twelve years. She found them in a cardboard box in the basement, the last, unfinished volume sitting on top. There wouldn't be much in that one—it would end March 14th at the latest. She picked up the book beneath it. A dark blue cover with large, lined pages and block-printed handwritten letters. She scanned the September entries. Midway she found:

> Jerome mentioned the meteors again. It's still eleven months off, assuming. His mentioning meteor showers made me think of Luna moths, those mammoth, fluffy, wonderful green monsters when I was a kid. Now the honey bees are going, the frogs, and maybe the butterflies, too. Probably haven't seen a shooting star since I last saw a Luna moth, unless you count that animated moth on the Lunesta commercial. I asked Marshall William's kid Arnie why that moth was in those Lunesta commercials and he said he had no idea. A fourteen year old who's never seen or heard of a real Luna month. And didn't seem to care. Why am I surprised? Still, it's a disappointment.

> Jerome says the meteors showers are usually well-timed even if some are better than others. So if I haven't seen a shooting star since I last saw a Luna moth, it's like going back in time. I frankly like the idea. But what will Samantha say? I'll have to think on that one.

Mrs. Harris stared at the page. First she felt anger, a fire in her fingers, the way anger often hit her. He was so cautious in his actions. "It's still eleven months off, assuming." He didn't mean assuming Jerome didn't change his plans, or the weather was bad, or there was a business emergency. He never *counted* on anything—including being *alive* the following August. Yes, he was right. But if she dug through these diaries, how many other things would she find he'd passed up without ever mentioning? Each morning, he saw the day ahead as nothing stronger than tissue paper. Harry knew he had an uncertain future. His father had died of heart disease at sixty, his grandfather at fifty-seven, an uncle at fifty-five, his mother at fifty-one. He was only fifty-two, but he already had the arterial stent Dr. Berg inserted in December. And, yes, in March, Harry keeled over one day simply walking through the warehouse, a victim of his DNA.

So, what was Mrs. Harris's future? Her garden and her garden club meetings, golf or tennis, furniture dusting, and the close reading of Harry's diaries to check for secrets? But she wasn't sure she wanted to know his secrets, including the trips they might have taken, but didn't. Revelations bore inherent dangers. Ignorance perpetuated the status quo. But the status quo meant that, some day, without any real change in the way she lived, it *would* be her funeral, not because of genetic misfortune, but simply because evil courses through well-ordered passive lives and thieves the beautiful. You could nurse and coax, but in the long run death was obstinate.

Harry had always enjoyed the Fourth of July. Maybe he really did want to see a meteor shower. Maybe he wanted them *both* to see the shower. Maybe.

On August 12th, Mrs. Harris woke to a day too fine to refuse. The sky was pristinely blue, with none of the usual D.C. "haze;" the temperature was seventy and headed to no more than eighty; and the humidity seemed piped in from Arizona. It had to be an omen if not even a commandment. Somewhere, Harry was still commanding, still arranging, still in control of the digital remote for the Sony plasma. But *she* would be the one to see the meteors, not him; and she would do it simply to please herself. That fellow Jerome might appear bland on the surface, but she was intrigued to hear he'd built his own cabin, that they would be heading for mountains with clear, dark evening skies, that they might relax on his deck drinking wine, while the atmosphere, shot by tiny pellets from space, conjured ephemeral, bright, phosphorescent-like streaks. The more she thought about Jerome's bland looks, the more comfortable she became and then, rationally or not, the more wary she grew over her sense of comfort. There could be mystery beneath the most casual appearing of people. But what shape would the mystery take? Surely he was no ax-murderer. But mystery didn't mean beauty. She wasn't going to be led about with cow-like passivity. For safety she'd start out conservatively, and let her trust work up until she was sure it was justified.

He arrived in an impossibly small car, a red Mini-Cooper with a white top and a large sunroof. He put her small overnight bag in the slim boot of the car. He asked what music she liked. "Classical," she said, not looking at him. She watched the road as he drove. She wanted to verify his driving habits. She'd constantly had to snap at Harry to brake, to signal, to use all three rearview mirrors.

"Okay, classical," Jerome replied, asking her to open the glove compartment.

They listened to Charles Martin Loeffler's *Pagan Poem*, a work Mrs. Harris had never heard before.

"Would Gustav Holtz be too corny after that?" he asked.

So Mrs. Harris loaded *The Planets*.

At the start of the drive, Jerome had asked if she minded him lowering his window a bit, and she said "a bit" was okay. He also asked if he might open the sunroof a bit, and yes, once again, "a bit" sounded safe.

But what would happen to this little car, despite the front and side air bags Jerome pointed out, if it encountered an SUV or a pickup?

"We'll just drive and enjoy it," Jerome said. A half-hour later, he opened the sunroof all the way. He glanced at Mrs. Harris who was peering intently ahead, looking uncertain as the air ruffled about them. "Better than air conditioning," said Jerome. "Pay attention to the road," Mrs. Harris remarked. "I don't mind the air, I just want to be sure this car stays on the asphalt."

The last half mile of the 110-mile drive was on a shale-and-gravel road top, passing through woods and then breaking into a large field with five widely-separated houses visible. Houses with acreage.

His, when he pointed it out to her, was truly nice, she realized. Maybe this trip would indeed suit, possibly in unexpected ways.

"Okay, just to be sure we put this issue to bed up front— pardon the pun," Jerome said as soon as they entered the cabin, "the downstairs bedroom is yours. Mine's the loft. I don't want you negotiating that circular staircase in the middle of the night, not really knowing this place like I do, even with two nightlights on. Both beds are queen-size, firm, and comfortable. We're not sleeping in cots, neither of us. Okay?"

Mrs. Harris stood in the indicated bedroom as he spoke. It was a back corner room, medium in size, well-lighted, and had an overhead fan. For that matter, nearly every living space in the cabin had a ceiling fan controlled by a remote. The bedroom had two nightstands, a large wicker trunk on which she could set her bags, a small clothes cabinet, and two ample closets. There were four windows, all with blinds. Despite a woodstove in the adjoining room, there was baseboard heating throughout the house. But it was summer, anyway.

More impressive, however, was the large, perhaps three-by-four foot abstract painting that dominated the room with the woodstove.

"You didn't paint this, did you?"

"No. I paint only walls and ceilings. Don't like it?"

"I like it very much," she said, startled to have said it. The room had a vaulted ceiling, not quite as high as the

room with the loft, but still very high. She also said she liked
the floor-to-ceiling stonework behind the woodstove.

He smiled. "They really do make sharp-looking artificial
fieldstone these days, don't they?"

She didn't believe for an instant he was putting her
down. She suspected he might be one of those people
uncomfortable at accepting compliments. How likely could
you call humility bland?

"Oh, a warning," he acknowledged. "The well water
has iron in it, so if you want drinking water, head for the
fridge."

They ate a sunset dinner at the Heights Restaurant which
peered over the valley where Jerome's cabin sat. Below
them ran the Potomac River, something she would never
have guessed. The Heights was an old and popular—though
expensive—restaurant about half-full when they arrived.
Even so, they got a window table. They didn't talk much.
Mrs. Harris did not admire Jerome's way of grasping a fork,
plus at times he ate with his elbows on the table. She had to
be honest with herself and keep her eyes open. Even if he'd
never been taught these things, working in D.C., shouldn't
he have noticed simply by example? There was no way she
could believe he never ate out.

Soon the sun dropped behind the mountains. Jerome
made a gesture to the waiter—raising a hand to "scribble"
an airy signature on an imaginary check. That gesture hadn't
been born of ignorance, surely. After paying, they drove the
three miles back to the cabin, neither saying a word.

It was after nine p.m. Lightning bugs flittered about almost
randomly, yet staying within ten or twelve feet of the
ground. Mrs. Harris had not seen a lightning bug since…
well, a long time.

She would have called Jerome's place a "cottage,"
not a cabin. It was too big, and had too much glass to be

a cabin. From within, the extensive use of glass gave a nearly continuous view of the area and neighboring houses. Some of the homes were large, including a few sizeable log cabins. Jerome's place sat on four acres of mostly open land, and from the long front deck, you could see mountains in Maryland, invisibly, from this point, overlooking the Potomac. Far off, she heard a train and the Doppler shift of the horn as the train echoed into the distance. An actual train running mountain passes.

"Well, want to sit outside?"

"Isn't it early? Didn't you say the meteors don't start till ten o'clock or even midnight?"

"Or three a.m., sometimes. But I've got a ratty old lounge chair and you can have this leather-backed chair. It's light and comfortable. And we'll put the little table between us and get some wine? Only two choices, I'm afraid, semillon-chardonnay, and merlot."

Mrs. Harris drank the semillon-chardonnay, since she'd never tried it before, and then simply listened. Crickets. All around them the needle-chirps of crickets. When the lightning bugs finally dispersed, Mrs. Harris heard an owl hooting, and then noted the deep swoops of dark birds, swallows or purple martins.

How long had it been since she'd ventured into "nature?" She and Harry usually took an autumn day's drive along the Shenandoah's Skyline Drive, but really never stepped out of the car, except to find facilities, or information, or a place to eat. They certainly never hiked. Sometimes they picnicked at Great Falls, where the Potomac cascaded over enormous rocks and the churn of the water was treacherous. Every year roughly a dozen people drowned, including kayakers practicing white water runs, and rock climbers who lost their grip and fell. Once an inverted kayak became caught in a washing-machine whirlpool, not even the strongest escaped. But Mrs. Harris only saw the waterfalls, never the disasters, and only the colored foliage of Skyline Drive. That and Luray Caverns, the underworld of unearthly colors.

Jerome had set a pad and pencil on one end of the small table that separated them. "I count and time them just for the hell of it," he told her. "Silly, but sort of fun."

They continued to quietly sip wine. The crickets continued their song. Mrs. Harris tried to remember daytrips she'd taken other than to Skyline, Great Falls, or Luray Caverns. Once she and Harry had taken an hour-long train ride through fall foliage in West Virginia, but it had been a dry year and the colors dull.

Mrs. Harris turned toward Jerome, plainly looking at him. Why had he invited her here? Was she indeed nothing more than a substitute for Harry, or a perceived obligation to the man who had discounted Jerome's building materials and offered him construction advice? In the dark, she noticed Jerome's face more surely. He had a surprisingly striking silhouette, a disciplined look, lost however to the silly act of sitting in the old green lounge chair whose bottom sunk so severely that his tail end nearly touched the deck itself.

"There, did you see that?" Jerome made a single pencil stroke at 10:44 p.m.

"No. Where? Is it gone? *Where* should I be looking again?"

Jerome repeated by pointing at a general area of the sky. "They'll all come from that source. Think of it as a beehive, though you can't see the hive, only the escaping 'bees'."

"Oh. Oh, there! Wasn't that one?" Mrs. Harris excitedly pointed.

"Yeah. I just saw the tail end of it." Jerome recorded 10:53.

They saw nothing the next hour. Both he and Mrs. Harris had closely tended their wines, Jerome saying there was more if needed. Mrs. Harris was beginning to wonder if the meteors were streaking all around them, but the wine had misguided her, making her miss too many. Once again, she begged reassurance on where to look.

Holding a half full glass of red wine, Jerome stretched an arm out, saying, "There—" at which point the bottom of his cloth lounge chair ripped fully open, dumping him and the contents of the wine glass rudely onto the deck.

"Well, I should have known better," he said. "It's been getting ready to go the better part of two years. I'll have to get another chair. Straight-backed and not very comfortable, unfortunately."

"But your jeans … they're soaked red. You'd better wash them."

"No washing machine, I'm afraid — the iron in the water. But maybe I'll go throw the jeans in the shower for five minutes anyway, and we'll see how that does." When Mrs. Harris absent-mindedly followed him with the intention of offering advice, he said, "No, you're the sky observer. Stay at your post. Enjoy this. What I'm doing now, changing pants, that's the everyday world …. Believe me."

He disappeared and soon Mrs. Harris could hear the sound of running water. After a while, Jerome turned it off and returned to the deck, wearing a fresh pair of jeans and carrying a plain, upright wooden chair.

"Anything?" he asked.

"No, I don't think so." She wondered if she'd been listening too much to the sound of the shower.

It was 12:15. "Well, you never know," said Jerome, just as Mrs. Harris was diverted by a grand streak of light that rushed across the sky. Jerome missed it.

At 12:55 things began to look up.

"Oh!" said Mrs. Harris. "Oh!" Eight passed within two minutes.

At 1:20 a.m. she said, "Oh!, oh!, oh!" repeatedly.

"God it's great, isn't it," said Jerome. "Sorry that Harry isn't here to see it."

"Harry?" said Mrs. Harris. "*We* see it, you and I, isn't that enough?"

She gasped and continued making sounds both smaller and larger as a nearly unending swarm paraded for a quarter hour. She'd set aside her wine, and leaned forward in her chair, looking delightedly for more.

"Uh-oh," Jerome suddenly noted, not sounding happy. "I think we've had it."

He pointed toward the river which couldn't be seen because it was too low and far away, but at 1:40 a.m., a curtain of fog was rolling up.

"Well, this happens," he said. "Christ, I'm afraid that's tonight's show."

A fog was slowly rolling straight up across the area of sky where the Perseids originated.

"How can you be sure? Mightn't it go away?"

"Yeah. Some time between eight or nine in the morning, usually. Sorry. Didn't mean for this to be a bust for you."

A 'bust' for me? Is that what he thinks?

"I've loved this, every minute," she said. "We may only have had a half hour of good viewing, but it was still … it wasn't the *ordinary*. I haven't seen a shooting star in years and tonight I saw fifty or more, in beautiful long arcs, in those last minutes alone. And though I knew you deeply honored your boss, Harry was prone to mechanics and efficiency rather than the appreciation of beauty." Then she paused. "Except if you read sections of his diaries. It's as if he was one sort of person as a child and then …" She couldn't finish the words.

When they went inside, she asked if she could see the view from the loft. Slowly, somewhat awkwardly from the wine, they ascended the circular staircase leading to the loft. Seventeen feet of glass covered the face of the original portion of the cabin, the part Jerome had finished first before adding the room with the woodstove and the back bedroom and later a kitchen on the opposite side.

"Well, there's a great view in daytime," Jerome exclaimed. "And if you keep this back window open, the air streams through while you're sleeping, true fresh air, even if that sounds corny. I like just staring at the field behind the house when the sun rises. It's all so golden."

Mrs. Harris took a measured breath. "Are you—" She stopped.

"Am I ...?" Her hesitation was obvious.

She couldn't look at him as she said it. "Are you gay?" she suddenly said. "I mean, were you, for Harry?"

Thinking on it, Jerome did not find her question implausible. "Well. Please don't take offense. I could dodge this, but I'm not going to. Frankly, though I learned a lot from Harry, I never *liked* him. To me, he wasn't like*able*. He was ... formal to the extent that ... he was standoffish. Not as if he didn't like a person, but as if he couldn't let himself get too close. He helped you, he had concern, but he didn't act *free*. I know that's impolite to say, but, given your obvious hypothesis, I think I need to say it. And no, I'm not gay."

"I'm forty-three," Mrs. Harris announced.

"I'm thirty-four," said Jerome. "Frankly, half the reason I stayed with Harry so long was to get glimpses of you. I wished you'd come to the office more often."

"We shall pay for this someday," she remarked. The bed felt wonderful.

"You're not too tired for this?" he said. Plainly he could see she wasn't.

"At some point in life," she remarked, "I realized Harry was gay."

"I wondered," Jerome replied. He'd said he hadn't liked Harry, and now he was about to bed the man's widow. Without thinking, he said, "I got the impression that Harry was deep-at-heart unhappy. Do you think if he—" He stopped. Would Harry have lived longer if he'd lived as he wanted? Out of the closet? He knew about Harry's family history of heart disease. Even so, could a fiercely honest change in lifestyle—stepping out—have made a difference? The question had no answer. And really what he cared about was this woman, not conjectures that could turn the evening's adventures into an intellectual exercise, ending anything of meaning or value. As he undressed her, Mrs. Harris stopped him just as he was about to undo the last button of her blouse. Curiously, she took hold of

his hand and held it toward the small Art Deco lamp still
lit on the nightstand. She saw the veins and roughness and
the strength that had come from building this cabin. Then
she saw the gash. A recent, not quite healed gash that might
have made it difficult for him to hold a fork 'properly.' These
weren't accountant's hands at all, she realized. "You have
strong hands, Jerome," she said, with a wonder in her eye.
With these strong hands, with nothing bland about them,
he touched her skin with definite, measured lightness as he
bent to her, moving infinitely more patiently than the lights
that had so graciously stroked the night sky only an hour
ago.

SCIENCE

All I can say is that she was a girl I'd met in one of my family's annual two-week midsummer sojourns to the farm where my dad grew up near Cameron, a small town in Northwest Missouri; that she and I lay with our backs to the ground and our hands behind our heads; and that we were looking at clouds. Watching them drift through the hot, blue sky, cumulous, with their heads bowed like the sails of eighteenth century tall ships under a full wind, or at least the way the movies depicted such ships, pirate ships, if you like, or man-of-wars. I was fifteen and so was she and it was summer, 1961, and the air was clear, in a time before most people ever heard of air pollution, even though vacations almost always meant by car, even from Richmond, Virginia, where my family lived.

"That one?" she asked, thrusting her chin at one. "And what do you think of it?"

"Head of cauliflower, I think."

"Not cotton balls? Cauliflower sounds so hard-edged, don't you think?"

"Are we talking shape, or texture? Don't they all look like cotton balls?"

"They all do look like they have the *feel* of cotton balls, yes," she agreed, "so we'll rule that out. No, what mystifies me is how you can see them over and over, and no two are alike."

"We'd get bored if they were," I noted.

"And what makes you sure that there aren't any two alike?"

She angled her body toward me, propped her head against a palm, elbow on grass.

"Are you trying to be difficult?" I responded. "You just said so yourself."

"Yes, but, are there, or aren't there?"

"Two clouds alike?"

"Yes."

"No," I said.

"Are you certain?"

"Yes."

"How do you know?" she challenged.

"Well, unless we're talking Coca-Cola bottles or cigarette packs, I think just about everything's different." I laid the words out as if proclaiming a maxim.

"You're saying all Coke bottles are alike?"

"Yes, generally."

"Generally? What's that mean?" She was pushy.

Now I turned my body toward hers, looking at her the way she was looking at me. Julie Hammersmith, my cousin Carol's friend I'd met at the Cameron pool two days ago. And later again that same day, near the bandstand. Their family had driven to my grandparents' farm for Sunday supper the day we began our cloud theorizing. Catfish and fried chicken and potato salad and Jell-O fruit salad and corn ears and watermelon all placed upon red-and-white checked tablecloths covering a picnic table and a card table. Folding chairs. After-church supper in the front yard, under the shade of two aged but yet sky-groping elm trees.

Afterwards, the two of us had trooped west of the house, past the chicken coop, past an aged and neglected tractor, past my grandmother's vegetable garden, past the long, long row of trees that served as a windbreak, to a place where we looked to be sure no cows had been, where we'd laid down and looked up, skyward.

She had pink lips and reddish, not quite red, hair—but not roan, either; freckles on her cheeks, especially under her blue eyes and across the bridge of her nose; an ounce of rosy fat, a gentle plumpness all over her, you could see it for sure in a bathing suit; and braces, which she was shy about, but not inordinately—it didn't stop her smiling. With her braces, the way she talked so energetically, it was nearly the same way as with her plumpness; you hardly noticed, almost as if the braces weren't there. What you knew was that regardless, this girl was pretty.

"Well, I guess," I said, thinking about it, "that under a microscope, you would find tiny differences between one Coke bottle and the next. I wouldn't think Coke bottles would be so identical at that level. Maybe chips in a bottle, or bubbles in the glass, or something so small it'd be a difference we couldn't even see in a microscope."

"That small? How do you know?"

She laughed. She was playing a game with me.

"How do I know?"

"Yes, Einstein, what's your proof?"

"Let's go back to clouds," I proposed.

"Why not Coke bottles?"

"Well, with clouds," I proffered, "there's always the wind. And at sunset, there's certainly the light, the red of the sun. But if there's a wind, I don't care how small, then, a cloud always varies. Even the same cloud changes in a breeze, right?"

"I don't know. I'm waiting for you to convince me. I could even ask you what 'the same cloud' means."

"Are you stubborn, or what?" I protested jokingly.

She laughed, with no visible concern for her braces. Then she smiled broadly with her lips closed. Pink, plump lips. I'd never kissed a girl before. She was making me wonder.

"No," she said, "prove to me that even if the wind changes a given cloud, that no other cloud anywhere else in history has looked just the same."

"You're not stubborn," I said, "you're obstinate."

She laughed again, making the sun glint off her braces for the briefest moment.

"Or don't you think I'm sane?" she teased.

"Right now I'm debating whether my cousin Carol is sane for having you as a friend."

"Right. Right. That's exactly what you're wondering."

"What is this? What is this we're doing?"

"Examining clouds, I thought," she asserted.

"Or Coke bottles."

"Let's stay with clouds for a while, like you said," she said.

"Okay. Does that mean we have to lie on our backs, or can we keep staring at each other?"

"You can stare at me if you want. I've let boys stare at me."

She'd *let* boys stare at her, or induced them to?

"Look. Are you a standard-issue farm girl? I'm East Coast, Richmond, Virginia. Every year, in the heat of summer, my family drives two days to get here, spends twelve days here at the farm where my dad grew up, then drives two days back. Maybe someday we'll get a car with an air conditioner. You met my dad's parents. In the farmhouse, they sleep downstairs and we get the upstairs bedrooms. Hot air ascends. But like I say, we're city-life Easterners. So is there some secret difference, living your life here on a farm?"

"How long have you been coming here for summer vacations?"

"Since I was three, I think."

"Then don't you know?" She giggled.

"I'm slow," I said, and pawed some grass and tossed it in the air in her direction. It didn't reach.

"Let's stay with clouds, like I said," she repeated, "but say we don't have to lie on our backs and *look* at the clouds. You can look at me all you want."

"What's your question?" I said, feigning annoyance.

"Let's say there was no wind. You said wind was one of the factors that made it impossible for two clouds to be alike. So let's cancel out the wind."

"How would we know there's no wind?" I prompted.

"Good question. Let's say we're meteorologists who've launched a balloon with a radio instrument package that signals there's no wind."

"Okay. So theoretically," I suggested, "the balloon ascends straight up, if we put aside the issue of the earth's rotation, if that affects whether the balloon goes straight up or what. But how precise is the instrument?"

"Oh, wow. You're getting tough," she responded. "Why do you want to know about that?"

"Well, maybe there *is* a wind, but it's so small, nothing registers."

"Then we've got a very inadequate science is all I can say," she declared.

"The science is inadequate, or the measurement?" I responded.

"Which is more important? Is the first dependent on the second?"

"Well, hold it now," I said. "All of a sudden I'm thinking there's the possibility that there could always be *some* wind. I'm not sure how you could prove otherwise."

"How do you mean?"

I sat stumped for a moment, putting a finger to my lips, waiting before I spoke. "Well, when you think about it," I said, "how can we be sure any two things are alike except for atoms?"

"Atoms?"

"Yeah, atoms," I repeated.

"So you think all atoms are alike."

"Sure. I mean, an atom of oxygen is just like another atom of oxygen."

She frowned at the same time she smiled. "Have you had chemistry yet? Do they teach it at your school?"

"Sure."

"Then have you forgotten about isotopes, where the same element, say, uranium, has different atomic weights, U-235 and U-238?"

"Oh. Yeah." She had me. I'd screwed up on that one.

"But you really had me going on that business about wind speed," she said.

"What do you mean?"

"When you asked how we can be sure there's never any wind. Discounting a vacuum, maybe, and cutting out considerations like the solar wind—which isn't what you meant by wind—you really asked a good question."

"Which is?" I wanted to hear this.

"How can we be sure there's no wind? How do we know a wind of 15 miles per hour isn't 15.001 miles per hour—and changing. You haven't taken calculus have you?"

"*You've* taken calculus?"

"Well, let's say I've just done some light reading. They don't teach calculus in high school around here, but my brother is a sophomore at Columbia."

"Columbia, Missouri, you mean."

"Of course. Here, that's what 'Columbia' always means."

"So he teaches you calculus?"

"No. I teach him from his textbook. He says I saved his behind."

"So what's calculus got to do with this?"

"It deals with rates of change. And that's perhaps what you're talking about. Sir Isaac Newton invented calculus. But maybe you could have, too."

"What?"

"If you thought and thought and looked at things closer and closer and closer, always checking for smaller and smaller differences," she said.

I'd had it. She was fooling with me. I lay back, looking for a cloud to stare at.

"You know what I'm going to get out of this?" I said.

"What?"

"Chigger bites. Nothing but chigger bites."

"Not quite," she said.

And then she leaned over and kissed me on the lips. She just right up and did it.

"So what have you learned now?" she challenged.

"I can feel your braces behind your lips. Your lips feel so plump, but I do."

She sighed a long sigh, leaned over me again, and kissed me again.

"Are you sure?" she said.

"No," I said. "I guess that one was maybe different."

THE LADIES IN WAITING

ONE

About two in the afternoon the doctor visited. The room was Spartan in its furnishings, and window curtains cut off much of the light. The five people in the room quite filled it up. The woman in the bed was small and ancient, china-white with blue veins and thin white hair and her breathing labored. The elder daughter's husband had brought in two chairs and placed them by the dresser so that both daughters could sit. The doctor had shaken everyone's hand when he'd come in. None had met him before. The doctor took the mother's chair, an old armchair upholstered in green. The elder daughter's husband stood near the window. The doctor was not an impressive man, not the model image for a doctor. He wore a rumpled sports jacket and he was overweight. He was in his late forties, possibly the age of the younger daughter.

The doctor told them that, within bounds, the whole thing would follow a standard order. He didn't think it necessary to closely examine the woman, who at ninety-two had spent almost three years shuttling between assisted living, where she was now, and nursing homes. No, there was nothing practical to do about it. Time was all. She might go today or she might go tomorrow or she might go the day after that. The daughters had already traded watch for a day-and-a-half, each promising to alert the other. Her limbs, the doctor said, might grow cold at first as the circulation retreated to preserve the vital organs. She was in a ragged but immensely deep sleep, and no, she was not likely to regain consciousness even for a short time. She was progressively bringing up mucus, struggling to breathe past the congestion. Gagging, though he did not say so. It would be congestive heart failure. And yes, the assistants were working to get a priest, but the priest on call could not be found. The staff would have to find someone else.

The doctor seemed comfortable making his statements. He was very certain and at the same time very kind. He worked for several assisted living centers, and it seemed as if he was relaxing from the shuffle of being constantly between here and there, at times breaking his speech just to sit and look at the patient, at the daughters. He may have sat for thirty minutes explaining this basically clear path that could be counted on. He would possibly be the last person to talk to them about their mother while she was still alive. Perhaps on some days he fretted about his disheveled state, that he would be the sore thumb on the photo of any hospital staff. Yet here he was setting to right the last hours or days together of these three women, the mother, her daughters.

Certainly he looked like he wanted to stay longer. Once again he told them no, as the other doctor had said the day before, the respirator wasn't a choice at this point. They'd done that a year ago at the hospital, when she'd first been administered the Last Rites. That had been a horrible experience for all of them, both the daughters and their husbands, including the husband not present today. On the respirator, the woman's entire face had been a frighteningly dark blue. She had a pulmonary embolism and the doctors were working catheters in and out. The two husbands talked. The body language of the younger sister's husband showed he didn't want to be there. His face at times bore a scowl. He constitutionally could not take seeing another person in misery, he asserted. Then the whole family was asked to join hands—the priest first telling the elder daughter's husband it was okay not to be Catholic—and the priest had administered the Last Rites. And that time she had lived.

By 2:30 p.m. the doctor rubbed his hands on his knees and rose. It was time to go. He wished everyone well. They said goodbye. The daughters had liked the doctor very much. They appreciated his frankness, even his homey, roughshod appearance. He was simple and direct.

The daughters now talked logistics. The husband looked out the window. What a fine day in June. The younger daughter had held the fort most of the previous day, and the older daughter most of today. Both lived fifty minutes from the assisted living center, one north, one south. Three years ago it had seemed a good compromise location, but in the end it labored them both.

The husband wandered out. He paced the floor, looking at this or that. He stared at the large fish tank in the main corridor. It was near his mother-in-law's room and the colors of the fish were nice so he lingered. He didn't like walking the hall even when he felt the need to pace. Nearby were the fifty-inch television and the two rows of chairs fronted by a floral-patterned couch. Four or five rag doll octogenarians with white hair, two tethered to oxygen bottles, lolled in the chairs. Sometimes the TV volume was loud, other times mute. But the rag dolls sat and blinked their eyes, focusing on something important, something pulling them to another center, and then to another center still.

He felt the tug on his arm. Standing made you bait. Politely he turned to face her. You don't remember me? I'm your Aunt Frances. Oh, but I've grown up and shame on you for not knowing.

An attendant diverted the woman. The safety of visitors as well as of residents.

He returned to the room. The three stared. The younger daughter went out briefly. The wife asked him if it made sense to get a room. There was a motel nearby. He said he'd do it.

He maneuvered down the corridor, past the drinking fountain to the elevator near the dining room. This was the third floor, the top. The floor not to be on. You had to be on guard near the elevator. Someone might be lurking, waiting for you to punch in the *321 code that would summon the elevator and let the hostages escape.

At 3:30 p.m. he registered in a Motel 6 and wondered if they'd ever actually use the room. They had no luggage at all.

Alone, the sisters made decisions. They agreed that the older would watch for now, that the other would return later. She was the one with the growing family to feed.

Driving back to the living center, the husband found a space in the front lot. As he approached along the stone walkway, he saw once again how nice the center looked. His wife had found it and the two sisters had settled the matter. A place that looked just like a house, large, with white siding and a green tile roof, and a pleasantly curving, gray-painted front porch with rocking chairs. On a day like today, a good June day and not yet four o'clock, five chairs were in use. Five ladies who smiled or nodded at you out of politeness, because they were pleasant people. Entering, he saw the big Labrador that followed one of the attendants about. The first floor held a semblance of normal life. He smiled at the attendant who greeted visitors and made calls to schedule hair appointments or to be sure your mother-in-law would be ready for a special two o'clock lunch excursion. Behind the greeting station was a large common room where church services were held, or games played, or entertainers brought in. Elsewhere a popcorn machine provided mid-afternoon popcorn. Nearby, a table in the sunroom offered plates of cookies. Ladies barely into their seventies sat comfortably in armchairs, turning the pages of paperbacks.

The husband patted the Labrador and punched the Up button. When the elevator arrived he pushed the third floor button.

What he hated especially on this floor, the floor with the Alzheimer's, the floor with the dementias, was the stink of toilet training gone awry. Assistants forever coming to clean up and all the toilets having high helper seats, as if for tall children.

He noticed a staff member sorting out two residents, each claiming the other had stolen her room. The virtue of patience.

His wife told him the sister had left to fix dinner. They sat in borrowed chairs, leaving the mother's chair, the more comfortable chair the doctor had sat in, vacant.

The mother was gagging on mucus. The wife fished in her purse for a pack of tissues. She sat on the bed and as her mother coughed the daughter wiped away the phlegm as best she could. She held her mother's face as if she were nursing a child. They—the daughter and her husband—had never had children. The husband watched astonished as his wife helped her mother, clearing away what shouldn't be there, clearing a path.

About ten p.m. the priest arrived. The two daughters and the husband and the priest all shook hands and introduced themselves while the mother's breathing labored on. The priest apologized for being so late. The daughters thanked him for coming. He administered the Last Rites. Everyone stared at the woman for a while. Well. The priest didn't want to interrupt them. Offhandedly, as the priest prepared to leave, the elder daughter asked the priest's name again, which he repeated. She asked whether he had a weekend cabin in a mountain development an hour away. He said he did. They talked for a half hour, the priest, the wife, and the husband. Yes, the priest had been in Rome but that was now several years ago. And no, he hadn't made it to community meetings in recent years. Thursdays were his cabin days. Weekends were God's time. Most of time was God's time. The husband and wife discussed the addition on their cabin. All three discussed the caretaker who cut the fields and maintained the roads and always had two or three cabin additions in progress. They stared briefly at the mother. The wife was very glad to have seen the priest. They all shook hands again as he left.

Past midnight the husband and wife discussed whether either should get some sleep. There was the unused motel room, after all. The three continued watching the mother, whose breathing was deep and ragged because she was choking, which tissue paper couldn't help. At one a.m. the husband drove to the motel. The ladies waited.

Just before one-thirty, the elder daughter nodded off for the barest instant. When she reopened her eyes, her sister told her the waiting was over.

An hour later a thought occurred to the elder daughter. She remarked that their mother had died on the date of her christening, ninety-two years before.

The next day, when the husband asked whether she'd had to close her mother's eyes, she'd said no. The difficulty, she'd said, was keeping her mother's mouth closed. This struck the husband as ironic. He'd been reading a book about the ancient Egyptians. The ceremony for the burial of pharaohs was called the Opening of the Mouth, to allow the dead to speak. The wife mentioned a note she'd found on the dining room table at the mother's house, now sold off, when she'd still been living there alone, never setting foot outside. "No glasses if there's a viewing." A stray note probably five years old. So the viewing was held with her face quite natural, though she had worn glasses all of her life.

TWO

The husband's grandmother's troubles had begun more than a year earlier, when at age ninety-eight she'd fallen trying to step around a woman in the dining hall line at her assisted living home. She'd broken her pubic bone, as a result spending four months in a nursing home fighting the attendants. She slapped their hands when they wanted to fiddle with her and she didn't want to be fiddled with. She complained and she barked. She was a small woman, but her skin was not pale, and her hair was grit-gray, not white. She was sturdy despite her defects. Her hearing was bad, yet hearing aids irritated her as much as helped, and usually went unused. Worse, parts of the world had now begun dissolving before her eyes. Macular degeneration had set in. She would leave the nursing home on a walker, but she would not fail to negotiate her pathway, despite her ears, despite her eyes.

Getting to ninety-eight had been a chore. At fifty, she'd been hospitalized for hemorrhagic pancreatitis. The husband remembered as a young boy being told he had to stay in the car while his parents visited, that children couldn't go in. Afterward, his mother said that the doctors put his grandmother's chances at fifty-fifty. The boy hoped. His grandmother gave great backrubs, baked fantastic coconut cakes, and played Chinese checkers with a flair.

At eighty she'd had a stroke which partially immobilized an arm. She did not stay depressed. She worked and reworked that arm for over a year. In her nineties she still kneaded back and shoulder muscles, going a good twenty minutes before quitting.

At eighty-two, she lost her husband of the same age to cancer. The funeral went fine, the grandmother never saying anything remarkable. Two days later, shopping, she kicked her grocery cart with a sharp foot and ran it into a stacked column of cans. Damn you to go first and leave me here alone. It was the end of the bickering that had enlivened their last twenty years together.

She entered assisted living at a Mennonite center when she was eighty-four. She was not Mennonite. She had a one bedroom apartment with a small kitchen and a living room that had a nice view of the grounds.

At eighty-eight, Bell's palsy caused one side of her face to collapse. It might go away, it might not. It did not. Every night she had to have one of her eyelids taped shut to go to sleep.

She turned nine-nine in mid-December, the year before her grandson's mother-in-law would die in June at ninety-two. For the grandmother's ninety-ninth birthday, the family had given a small party. She was now profoundly deaf and macular degeneration progressively closed off more of her world. When the grandson asked whether she thought her deceased husband might be watching, she smiled at such a naïve notion.

The next June, when the wife's mother passed away at ninety-two, the husband's grandmother began seeing monkeys in chandeliers. On the ceiling. On the walls. Medications were changed to no effect. In August she began to weaken. She was placed in a newly built nursing center. This time she accepted it.

In late August, there was a redirection of the family's attention. In September, the husband's niece was to be married in Cyprus. Though much of the family was going, the husband and his wife could not.

In early September they visited his grandmother at the nursing center. Some days she was alert and strong and other days not. They found her, the nurses said, on a good day, sitting in a rocker, not rocking, but alert. She could see who it was if she managed to tilt her face the right way. He had to speak right in her ear. Behind the house, the old cherry tree, your cherry pies. The Roman candles on the Fourth of July. With her palms up, she raised both her arms to shoulder level and set them down again. The endless supply of hard-shelled crabs you could always pick so fast. Again she raised and lowered her arms. What can you do? What can you do about any of it? Not listless shrugs. The sign language of acknowledgement.

She died in mid-September, two days after the wedding in Cyprus. The wedding party flew back for her funeral. Her sixty-five year-old son, one of those who had not gone to the wedding, arranged everything with the funeral home, picking the coffin, meeting the chaplain. It all went well.

Three months and a day short of one hundred.

Long afterward the husband said to his wife that it seemed as if his grandmother were still out there someplace, on a life raft, drifting at sea. Not dead at all, just drifting alone, forever floating but unfound.

THREE

Everyone thought the ceremony for the husband's cousin, a woman of fifty-two, had been nice. This was in late July, at a small Episcopal church a two hour's drive for many family members. A woman who had been a close friend of the cousin gave testimony to the deceased's visions of heaven. At the hospice, in her last days, she had described how she could see heaven so clearly, how she could see it with certainty. The priest read the traditional texts, but he also spoke beyond the traditional texts. He mentioned the morphine. He spoke of seasons and harvests at the same time that he spoke of the resurrection.

The husband's wife had liked it. The resurrection as metaphor, take it literally or take it as the earth in its rotation about the sun. It may be true or we may choose to believe it is true or we may choose to see it as one way of getting through.

They were walking across the gravel parking lot to their car, the reception at the church now over, the day reaching into late afternoon.

As if disclosing a secret, the wife added, And everything's in progress for number four. It is said that it occurs in threes, but the counting never stops.

The husband made no comment. He pressed the remote key to unlock the car.

As he started the engine, she said, I'd like to take a different route back. Do you mind? I think we're only an hour or so from the ocean here. We could drive with the windows down. Open the sunroof, too. What do you think?

He pointed to the glove compartment.

We need a southeast road if you can find one on the map. Or east, and then south. Everything out here is two lanes and full-out straight ahead. It makes you want to drive fast, but then you're always caught behind some farmer on his family's weekend outing.

Pass, pass, pass, she said.

As he drove, the air slipped in and upon and about them. His wife's hair windsocked. In the flat of the eastern coastland they passed vegetable and fruit stands, customers with their loop-handled paper bags filled with beans or peaches ready to be weighed by teenage girls efficiently counting money. They passed farm houses where dogs barked or chickens meandered in white clutter. At some, the long and slowly moving metal wands of modern irrigation systems brought water to crops.

The gift of small miracles: not a single car, truck, or tractor they needed to pass.

In an hour-and-a-quarter they met the coastal roads. The declining sun, falling upon the mountains well beyond the western horizon, burnished the right side of their faces as they turned southward. Immediately, they began to pass grass-tufted sea dunes, interrupted here and there by back roads that cut to residential properties, expensive, with ocean views. And then here and there, the occasional wide view of it, the huge black bulk of sea.

For half an hour they drove this way, enjoying the color of the evening sky, its blushing veins of high cirrus tangled with the salt smell of the Atlantic, neither of them saying a word. The wife's eyes gleamed when she turned to him and stroked the side of his head. Even in its going down, the sun looked as if it would last forever.

ANNA'S HEAD

*"... on a table in the shed ... the intact head ... the
lovely face ..."*

—Tolstoy, *Anna Karenina*

A s a teen living in Taiwan in the sixties, I once saw a
man who'd lost his head.
        It's hard to think that a head could be just one
part of a sequence of body parts—four or five disparate
segments that had once been a man. In our taxi, my two
friends, sitting on the driver's side, had the better view. The
oddity that stays with me when I think back on it, was not
so much the head, looking surprised or calmed in this or
that direction, as that the man's pants, his socks, whatever
clothing he'd chosen that morning, had all been pulled off,
too—as if he were a nude man who'd lost in his race against
the naked force of the train.

Why is this death—a decapitated, nude man—so much
more than another death? Why does it bring to mind the
patient who once asked me, "Can the soul be mocked?"

It is, I think, a question that I shall never escape. The
image of that headless man resides in my brain at some
level always, as if he were staring at me.

I sit alone at breakfast in a passenger ship cruising from
Baltimore to Quebec and back—a shipload of Americans.
It is late October. The weather is bad. We have just left

Halifax, Nova Scotia, which not two weeks before had been irreverently knocked by a hurricane. The city's parks are filled with huge, uprooted, fractured trees. The captain has left port early, heading east for Sydney, Cape Breton Island. We are outracing a storm, apparently. One we cannot see.

The breakfast room is crowded to overflowing. I'm finishing my last bites of muffin, re-reading Tolstoy's *Anna Karenina* knowing all too well the novel is building to a railroad "accident," where the subject of attention will be an "intact head," a "lovely face," bearing a certain expression. From that head and face Tolstoy forged a miraculous novel, at all points sympathetic and honest, and set upon the most elemental of human pursuits: love, happiness, the meaning of life. What more could I want, even in a re-reading?

I am about to turn a page, when I feel a slight compression of space.

"Excuse me, please. Sir?"

The breakfast room is a constant menagerie. Passengers fight for this or that table or seat, even if the morning will be spent at sea, no need to rush to make a particular booking. Still, who wants to stand holding a tray while someone sits merely reading. I look up expecting to make my apologies and relinquish my seat, which is only right, as I've finished even my tea.

But instead it is one of the young ladies bussing tables. I start to hand her a finished plate.

"You're reading this book, sir?"

Obviously, I'm reading the book. It's open to page 481. So I try to read her instead. She is pretty, she is young, she is polite, and strangely intrigued by what I am reading.

"Yes, I'm reading it."

"And you like it?"

She has unusual eyes, dark and quite beautiful, filled with a quiet sense, I think, of concentration, perhaps appraisal. Prideful, too, I warrant.

"Yes. I certainly like it."

She leans toward me, as though about to divulge a secret. "You don't see many Americans reading a book like this. *The Da Vinci Code*. Mysteries and thrillers. But *this*"— she taps page 481 with her left hand and its very naked ring finger—"is a book that will last for all time."

I turn in my seat and face her directly. I know that most of the young women serving as contract workers on the vessel are Russian. I know they will be gone from their homeland for months. I also know that for them it is good money. Long days of hard, constant work for money they cannot earn at home.

"Are you Russian?" I ask.

"No, I'm Romanian, but I know Russian. Did you know the Americans changed Tolstoy's name? He's Lev Tolstoy, not Leo. They changed it simply because Lev sounded unfamiliar."

"Yes, I know the name was changed. But I don't know who actually did the changing. Perhaps it was the English."

She begins clearing my place.

As I stand, she says, with no further explanation, "I am glad."

Were I to tell her the truth, I would say that I am glad, too, but I have thirty years on the young lady, and a frame of mind that constantly assesses and crushes from consciousness any speculation of unlikely worlds.

Yet now she lightly touches my sleeve. "Do you like ice cream?" Her eyes—are they not like dark chocolate ice cream? "I am dishing at lunch." She has piled cups, bowls, saucers, onto a tray she is lifting. Of course I like ice cream, though I merely stare. Utensils gathered, a single ice creamy glance, and she is moving away as others verge to claim my vacated table.

"Good day," I say, whether she hears me or not.

An hour later I find my friend Greta. She suggests we walk a mile on deck. We're both dressed for it, she observes. She clutches my arm and half-steers me through the main deck doors.

Outside she mysteriously runs her hands over my arm. "Robert, are you putting on weight?"

"Do arms gain weight?" I retort. "Good thing you're not grasping elsewhere."

She teasingly reaches for a love handle, and I slap her arm in sham defense.

It is cold, and we both feel it. The sea is not severe, but worsening. We have midday expeditions planned for Sydney, but I am sure we are both beginning to wonder.

My friend Greta is my friend Greta. We're almost, but not quite the same age. I've raided half my fifties, but she keeps a slim lead on me.

Walking on deck, I tell her about my Romanian.

"*Your* Romanian," she says, having heard me out.

"You know what I mean," I say.

"It's no different with you than any other man," she says. "You take childish pride in your presumption of a *potential* conquest, though you'd pooh-pooh any suggestion you would ever think such a thought."

"You're speaking of men in the same way my young Romanian was speaking of Americans."

"All the worse for you," Greta says, "because your Romanian pal and I are both right."

Greta and I have a long history. For years, she was a stringer on the local paper, while her husband ran a poodle parlor. Not precisely money-making enterprises. She had some insurance money—double indemnity—that came from the accidental death of her parents (yes, a freak rail accident—you see how this is going) when she was still young. Long ago she and her husband Ed—Greta and Ed Boschnägel—bought five or six properties, sat on them until the value grew unsightly, sold them, and socked the money away in various pockets. Five years ago they bought a timeshare in Puerto Rico, and actually had the pleasure of using it once.

I change the subject. "So, I didn't see you yesterday—not after the Halifax tour. Couldn't find you for dinner. Writing poetry in some secluded space? Not your cabin, I know, because I knocked three times."

She stops dead in place to look at me. "Tell me, Robert, do you always answer a knock at your door?" Her expression is serious, but she is joshing me.

"Yes, and loudly, if it's a cabin steward and I'm not dressed."

"No, I was not in my cabin. I wasn't in anyone's cabin. But, yes, I was writing. No laptop, just pen and paper. It was going well, and when it goes well I don't stop. I just found a space and stayed there. And don't ask where. We preserve our secrets."

Yes, we must work to keep our secrets. Work hard, work daily.

Though poetry, I think, in its way, reveals secrets—another's glimpse of the world, even the soul. Years ago Greta switched from writing newspaper articles to poetry, unassuming but interesting pieces, until Ed, diagnosed with ALS—"Lou Gerig's disease"—deconstructed in less than a year. I visited often in his final days. That was three years ago now. Overnight Greta's poetry changed, becoming—not somber—but simply more pensive, more deliberate, more patient—and more noticed. She won awards. She gave readings. Me? My brother was the editor who paid her next-to-nothing for her work on the local paper. I've known her twenty-plus years. Last year I spent a week at her timeshare. This year, we decided to outrun hurricanes in the not quite far north. Who, I ask you, would have thought there could be hurricanes in Nova Scotia?

Two weeks after the hurricane—and with some new storm apparently lurking—ours is a cold walk. As we approach the bow we find the crew has roped it off. "SEVERE WINDS," the sign says. Crossing the bow is always the best part of these walks. I enjoy feeling like a bird flying backwards in a gale.

I tell her it's no fun if we can't cross the bow.

She's got a massage scheduled in a little over an hour, she says. Given the cold and wind, we make contingency plans to rejuvenate ourselves later at the forward bar, the Seawall Lounge. Three p.m., we agree. If Sydney is delayed—or (worse) canceled.

An hour later I'm carrying *Anna Karenina* with me to the fantail bar which sits overlooking the tarpaulin-covered swimming pool. The deckchairs are all stacked, the cushions placed in piles. The ocean is now visibly choppy. As I'm sure the pool would be, too, if we could see it. Sea spray puddles the deck.

At ten a.m. the fantail bar is crowded with women. I find what must be the last seat. A cosmetics expert is giving a talk on skincare. She walks around trying lotions A and B and C on everyone. She includes me. My skin is too dry, she says. She uses an exfoliant and now I feel gritty. Given the crowd, it's impossible to read my book, and most of the time impossible to hear what the woman is saying, not that I want to listen.

The cosmetician looks like the grownup version of a girl I knew in Taiwan. We were all "military brats," not counting those whose parents were CIA. She (the girl in Taiwan) couldn't have been more than fifteen. We shared a pedicab ride in Taipei. I can't remember where we were going or why. It was in the rainy season, so the pedicab's front flap was buttoned up to keep the rain out. I ran my hand along her back twice, her neck, too, I believe, then stopped. She was plump. Under my hands her back felt wide, like a swimmer's. She looked at me. Why did I stop? Because to do more with someone imperfect might be expressing something stronger than a transient urge? Silly what thoughts we have at such a young age. Greta would comment on that. It might even make it into one of her poems—assuming I ever mentioned it.

But even indecision seems a sin. So many things seem sins.

When I was sixteen and our family returned home from Taiwan we carried a stack of books—including a complete *Britannica*—bought on the cheap, since all the books were pirated. Taiwan, like China, ignored copyright laws. But I never read *The Ugly American*, part of our pirated booty, until we'd returned to the States. *The Ugly American* was a bestselling novel about how other people—specifically, Asians—saw us.

Were we the ugly Americans? I'm not counting the time a bunch of kids climbed the barbwire fence behind our house to loot a Chinese cemetery, carting off skulls on bamboo poles. That event—that *travesty*—occurred a year before we got there. It's the other things, the things you were in control of, or should have been, that make you think.

My friend Jim had been held behind twice in school and was older than me though in the same grade. Jim was fearless and independent. We constantly traveled about Taipei without paying a dime. (NT actually, Nationalist Taiwan dollars.) The Taiwanese did everything by bicycle. The pedicab is an example: like a rickshaw pulled by a bike. But you'd see middle-aged men—in their forties certainly, perhaps their fifties—hauling extraordinary loads on what amounted to flatbeds pulled by bikes. Enormous loads of logs, ungainly piles of furniture strapped into place, hefty loads of cement bags. Dressed in T-shirts and shorts, these men strained yet continuously peddled—their calf muscles bulging, exhaustedly climbing any hill imaginable, because their lives depended on jobs meant for oxen.

That's how Jim proved resourceful. In the heart of Taipei, no matter where we were, he'd spot a man carrying a load that was not quite complete, and we'd hop on. Like getting a free pedicab ride. Sometimes the man would turn and look at us, not saying a word. A few blocks later, Jim would tell me to hop off. Then we'd find another cart heading where we needed to go, and hop on again.

The sins of the young—are they just naïve explorations? Callous stupidity or indifference?

Engraved in gold, you'll find Jim's name on the Vietnam Memorial.

Lunchtime arrives with no sign of Sydney. We'll either arrive late, or not at all. Greta is wherever Greta is, and I'm on my own.

As usual, they have set up the ice cream booth near the fantail. Three deep, steaming cold tubs, vanilla and always two surprises. But I am not trying to read the names of the flavors, but rather to control my lately inexperienced autonomic system.

"Ah," my Romanian says, reaching for a dish, "the man from room …?"

Um. "… Four fourteen," I say, feeling rather like a spy passing a code word. Possibly I am biting my tongue. She seems to be waiting for me to say something. I forget she is holding a scoop in her hands and that three other passengers wait behind me. Another server, a young man with blond hair, is scraping for another passenger the last of … I squint at the writing on the card … the tart lemon mint.

"The tart," I say, inexplicably, since they're now out of it.

My Romanian friend digs into the chocolate, ignoring my foolish faux pas.

"I thought you said you never ate dessert before two o'clock," she notes, handing me a dish with two well-formed mounds.

"I thought they stopped serving ice cream at one-thirty."

"That's true," she says.

I am a maze of stupidity.

Two minutes after two there is a rap at my cabin door.
When I open it, I see both the girl and behind her,
carrying a pile of linen, Gregor, the ship's steward—young,
his face scarred by acne—who cleans my cabin. She ignores
him.

"I have five minutes," she says, and closes the door on
poor Gregor. "Don't worry about Gregor," she says.

She is unbuttoning her blouse.

"Five minutes?" I say. *Five minutes?*

"Tops," she says. Her blouse is gone and then her bra, in
less than twenty seconds.

I want to admire yet I feel as if I am being guided by a
digital timer, as though a microwave were counting down
my allotted five minutes, when what I *see* is all analog in
nature, sweeping flesh, made illusory by circumstance.

She is gesturing with her fingers, a where-is-it gesture,
uttering something impatiently.

"You don't have anything?" she says.

Ah. "I wasn't expecting to need anything."

"It's not your needs. It's my needs." Did she say that?
Did I say it?

Now her shoes, too. It's all gone in a pile, clothes such
feeble matter—is she asking for a rubber? Did she ask me to
"rub her?"

I remember once a girl tugging on my belt, tugging in a
tug-of-war, a good game when you have time. But this was
chess played against a clock.

I know how ridiculous men can look in shoes and socks
and shorts, but shortly the shorts went, too. Time, time! The
godless angel of precision instrumentation—the guiding,
grudging preeminence of time.

"We'll do a Bill Clinton," she is saying. "It's faster."

I know that she is thinking logistically and I am not
thinking at all.

She smiles and says, "This way if they ask if we had sex, you can say 'No.'"

I am embarrassed. She is making me grow. How long have I been on the wagon? Four years?

"How old are you, anyway?"

More stupidity. Ask a question, she has to stop what she is doing to answer.

"Twenty-four. How old are you, anyway?"

"Fifty-six. You're going to kill me, you know."

"Hmm. My very own human sacrifice."

Her hair is back. Every button buttoned. She examines her lipstick in the small bureau mirror.

"When you disembark in Baltimore," she says, "you will put thirty dollars in Gregor's envelope—that's the standard tip for a steward. But you will add an extra fifty for me. I trust you. You are a good boy, you lover of literature. As for Gregor—he is a very dependable sort, just as human and honorable as Kafka says despite his looks."

It's now 2:45. I sit in the Seawall Lounge, reading *Anna K.*— I have now crested page 525—drinking a double-malted whiskey, very smooth, early for my 3:00 p.m. contingency get-together with Greta. When she arrives, I will switch to wine to keep her company. My pulse is quite regular, my mind returning everything to the way it was before my Romanian's arrival.

Unthinking of my Romanian makes me think of Greta. Reading *Anna Karenina* does the same.

I've learned a great deal from Greta. In twenty-odd years, she has always given me peace of mind. This started before she was Mrs. Ed Boschnägel, but not overly long before. Greta was quite an attractive young woman. Someone who distracted even the most conventional, the most self-regulating of men. When I first met her, it was as if the physical world were on fire, the steam rising everywhere

around her, as if she had just stepped off a train in one of
those old movies—am I thinking of *Brief Encounter?*

We met at one of my brother's occasional standup
dinners. This particular feast—a mid-afternoon affair—
sprawled from his gargantuan stainless steel kitchen to
the springtime world of the great old backyard barbecue,
hell's own belching hatchery of heat and smoke. Greta's
face gleamed, then vanished, then reappeared through the
shimmering background of scorched air and milling people.
Each time I saw something new, yet sensed something
intriguingly familiar—the indefinable déjà vu. As it turned
out, Greta and I were two came-alones. I had not come in
a good frame of mind. A colleague had been shot the day
before by a distraught patient. A madwoman—to use a term-
of-art—whose bullet had shattered my friend's collarbone
before it ricocheted and struck a wavy Dali hung too close
to several diplomas. I was riding a train of thoughts. And
here this woman—Greta—emerged from the steam.

But atmosphere and circumstance do not construct
mystically in the space before you a wholly new person, a
mesmerizing central character in your life, as long as you are
aware of atmosphere and circumstance. But I wasn't. I liked
her, I first thought, because she avoided certain frivolous
sorts of comments I so often heard upon being introduced.
Not, "Oh, dear, I'll have to watch what I say." Not, as
another woman once elaborately concocted, "Well, I won't
ask whether you've ever fantasized being Montgomery
Clift in *Suddenly, Last Summer*, as you'd probably say, 'Only
in comparison to being Montgomery Clift in *A Place in
the Sun*.'" I told that woman—who did not remind me of
Elizabeth Taylor—she'd left out *Raintree County*. We doctors
of the mind are *not* always evaluating, assessing, no matter
what stereotypes movies or TV or magazines—and through
these, people at large—assign us to.

Greta took one look at me and asked if I ran. I said I did.
"Marathons, or casually?" she wanted to know. She was

drinking white wine. I still recall the dance of sunlight in her wineglass, its refractions playing on her face when she raised it to her lips.

"Sometimes marathons," I said, awkwardly trying to swallow a bite of hotdog, "… um …" (I'd finally swallowed it) "but if so, casually."

"So, what's casual?" she asked.

I said four hours twenty minutes or so.

"Does casually mean comfortably?"

"Not particularly. Is this an inquisition?"

Without hesitation, she said, "I run five miles a day at whatever pace feels comfortable. Until my mind becomes my body for a while and pace is all there is."

It sounded somewhat pretentious. "Are you into biofeedback theory?" I asked, fearing this might turn into one of the gamesmanship introductions I too often encounter.

"No. Are you? And do you always bring a book to parties?"

I cradled a book under an arm. A thick book.

"You never know about parties," I said, caught.

"Do you mind? I'm always intrigued to see what people are reading."

I showed her the volume.

"You might want to consider poetry," she said. "Thinner. Easier to hide." She smiled and leaned forward as if to convey a secret, briefly touching my arm. "Sorry, but if we'd continued where we were going, we'd now be comparing Nike with Reebok."

She was coy. A touch on the arm is a tactic. But still.

"So, what happens when you're not running? Do you enjoy your work?" I asked.

"Have you ever worked for your brother?" she joked, smiling again, this time knowingly, engagingly. "But I fly-fish, too." She compared the back-and-forth silver-white casting of the line, the associated articulation of wrist and arm, to the meter of a poem. She made me see the fly-fisher standing in waders amid pellucid, cool streams, bedeviling trout with the intricacy of a well-fashioned fly.

Had she caught me already, I shall always wonder—the pace of running, the rhythm of a poem, the silver-white cast of a fishing line: were pace, rhythm, and movement her mantras? Or was it her face? She had trained her gray, long-lashed eyes on me in an irrevocably disarming way—a graceful quality you do not immediately see as a smile— one that lies behind the abundant and obvious smiles she willingly gives, something unrealized until you are alone and think and suddenly see.

She said she was a farmer's daughter from Iowa. I told her I'd never met a farmer's daughter. Her eyes lit from a private humor. "Around here? In a city of lobbyists, lawyers, and lawmakers? No one's met a farmer's daughter."

Out of a backyard barbecue, steam billowed and swallowed me up.

So, for the two months or so before there was Ed Boschnägel, we sometimes found time for a run. Once she found her pace, to see Greta run was to see something fully self-actualized. Then her head ran level in the air, her arms gliding infinitesimally in course with the rest of her, her motion as synchronous as a pendulum, her heart and her mind one. And once—once only—there was the post-run shower scene, the unexpected gift of recreation on a plane of dark carpeting. All during which I looked at her face, at her eyes looking desperately back, knowing we were at the edge of her pace, at the want of her pace, so close to it, so very near. Then suddenly there was a gap, wasn't there, her eyes drifting from mine, and the gap widened, so that I could see in her distracted face what I recognized in the lost ambition of her now barely rising hips—I had to watch as the animal within her somehow slowly escaped.

It seemed I could run with Greta, just not all the way.

After that, for another month, we still found time for the occasional run. And I recognized her pace when she fell into it. I could see her head riding as wholly, naturally level as ever—unchanged and unchanging. And then I had to stop, just stop, stop in the middle of the run, our last because I made it so, because when she found her pace it occurred because it occurred, not a minute of it owed to me.

Though I hadn't quite yet given up thinking—imagining—a different fate. It is hard to say to yourself—to admit—there's no going forward.

Hurt happens in many directions. Early in life I set a rule not to bed women I had no intention of seeing again. But more than once, I have, of course. The Romanian expedition surprised and unambiguously pleased me, but it has nothing to do with the rule I'm talking about.

I once went to bed with a very overweight woman whose one great talent was that she could massage a back. I am a sucker for a back rub. That night I foolishly asked her out to dinner again the following weekend. As dinners go, it was awkward, but she didn't know that. I walked her to her apartment, but didn't step in when she unlocked her door. Then she realized, of course. Involuntarily her arms flailed at the air, not actually grasping me, but *wanting*. She grimaced, panicky, her teeth gritting visibly, her whole face a portrait of desperation. Though I'd broken no promise, I had destroyed her peace. My punishment is remembering this woman, visualizing her arms clawing the air, her desire turning to helpless indignity. It remains to this day a considerable sin. I catalog it with the rest, but some carry a higher hurt than others.

Then, of course, time continues ahead, until the mind is filled with re-readings of *Anna Karenina*, and—if you're me—all the workday monologs of damaged people.

Until age accompanies you like a curious friend, and you wonder how you are still here. Until you're nearing sixty, and deck walking is such a compromise with desire.

But I had been speaking of Greta's gifts.

I learned haiku from Greta, or at least the principle of its form:

Five syllables first,
seven to cull attention,
five to make it leap.

To frame little pictures in the mind. Small and compact and quiet. This was before she began writing poetry, though she read much. The odd thing about haiku is that it was often written by warriors, yet the aim is a moment's sustained reflection. Thus the contradictory image of the warrior-poet, or poet-warrior, depending on how you see it.

I have tried several of the arts in my life. Watercolors, water-whirls of paint on canvas. I once took up sculpting. First I carved wood, creating a good many shaving piles. I have walked many miles with my hand-carved walking sticks. Then limestone, which I know deteriorates out-of-doors, but so much deteriorates over time anyway. I became rather skilled at sculpting the human form. I became adept at sculpting heads. Greta can tell you. Twenty years ago I sculpted hers.

My watch reads 2:55. If Greta is on time—which she always is—I have five minutes to kill.

But I am thinking of heads. Greg Bear's *Heads*, for instance, a storage locker of cryogenically frozen heads, saved for eventual revival and reattachment to a convenient body. But there have been so many heads of interest. The "dime lady" whose head graced the noble ten-cent piece in the early twentieth century was Mrs. Wallace Stevens. Yes, *that* Wallace Stevens. The poet whose wife had such a lyrical face. The wife the poet seemed never to want to talk to, yet never outright abandoned, never consummately betrayed. Or Iris Murdock's *A Severed Head*. Why do we make such a fuss over divorce? It's common, very common. I see the detritus of marriages every day. I hear of little else. Yes, of course, divorce is a form of death, a legalized killing, but being precisely that, it's not a crime. Iris Murdock's head was severed, too, in a way, by God, by the fates, by the mind's long vacation that is Alzheimer's. I knew she had lost it when I read *The Green Knight*. Such a ridiculous book. But so very many are. Love, marriage, affairs, the many forms of deceit: It is all *The Kreutzer Sonata* or *The Good Soldier* being played and replayed. And *Kreutzer* came from the pen of my revered Tolstoy. Even death is overplayed in literature. Try reading that novel by Reynolds Price, *The Promise of Rest*. Repetitious, unnecessary agony—a ghastly book, a monstrous misjudgment that it was published.

Any of these makes me wonder about the sense or senselessness of grief, when we have the choice to get on with our living. Unless the book is truly superb artistry: *Anna Karenina,* or *To the Lighthouse*. What we need more of is removal of grief in actual life—and doing that may take courage in unanticipated—at times even unknown, and securely secretive—ways.

"Well, you're looking in the pink," Greta says, settling into the booth. It is precisely 3:00 p.m.

"I am?" What's that mean?

"Goodness. You're practically blushing."

"Frankly, I thought *you* looked in the pink. The wonders of your morning massage."

"Oh, God no. Quite the opposite."

Am I blushing? Actually it is two minutes past three. An hour past my ice cream elaborations.

But Greta is already onto something else. "So," she says, straight-forwardly, "No Sydney."

"Says who?" I ask, raising a finger to the waitress, ordering.

"My masseuse."

"Um. Ship's company. Likely she knows. I'd been looking forward to Sydney."

"Sydney in particular? Why?"

"Could have gone to Australia for R&R in the seventies when I was in Vietnam, and didn't. Went to Hong Kong instead. Foolish decision. Woman in a leopard skin dress showed up at my door within five minutes. Five."

"And you didn't."

"Of course, not. Anyway, after that, 'Sydney' just sounded so much better, even if you put it in Nova Scotia and added pursuit by an invisible storm."

Two chardonnays arrive. Plus a refill of Chex mix.

We each take small handfuls to munch.

I watch her eat. She seems so perfectly at ease. Once upon a time I cared so deeply for Greta. What is a friendship, anyway? What do you lay down for the sake of it?

If only Greta had not loved animals, I would never have met nor needed to ask whether Ed Boschnägel was my friend. He was forty when I—when *Greta*—met him. The thirty-five-year-old Greta that I knew was half-animal, something gliding through nature. How did that link to Ed, who couldn't run two steps without looking foolish? I'm six feet, but he was gangly and taller, more limbs to him than he could coordinate. He was heavily balding and in a summer sun ran his hands over his pate as though in a perpetual quandary. He was, I think, incapable of guile. He looked awkward and helpless near people. But with animals—it's not that they were his support system; they were his life. And that, of course, spelled the difference. A man who could manage nothing more complex than other people's pets found a woman immersed in the idea of another's needs, of a soul devoted to lesser, even more helpless, creatures. Whether or not Greta—the farmer's daughter—had found her pace with Ed, she found her place with him.

So, what do you sacrifice for the friend of a friend? You sacrifice any thought of your own needs and commit to what could not have been yours anyway.

"Damn these cramps," she says momentarily and grimaces. At our ages, she certainly doesn't mean menstrual. "Another urinary tract infection."

"Another?"

"For as long as you've known me, Robert, I've had urinary tract infections. It's hardly the first time I've said it. Kills sex. You've known, but forgot. Damn it, Robert, sometimes I wonder if you ever pop outside of yourself."

There's nothing to say, so I wait for this squall of hers to disappear. In a minute, it does.

"So, two things, Robert," says Greta. "Forgetting any attempt on your part to impress a twenty-something Romanian, I realize you're reading *Anna Karenina* again, so I wonder why. I remember you were reading it when we first met. You even brought it to your brother's party."

"Oh, really?" Though a good book at a boring function provides an invaluable defense, had *that* been the book under my arm?

"And—as an extra added bonus—how's that book you're writing coming along?"

I smile. "Not as nicely as your poems, I expect."

"I imagine philosophy is not something easy to write," she interjects.

"And you never wrote a philosophical poem? Never mind, that's rhetorical. I haven't read *Anna Karenina* as many times as you might think. I'm a slow reader. I take my time. This is my third reading—you're sure I was reading it when we met? I'd never have believed that. As for why I read *Anna Karenina*, I think it's for a personal reason that occurred when I was very young." I tell her the story of my friends and me in the cab, crossing the railroad tracks in Taiwan. "I wanted to know this man's secrets. How he had come to meet his death with a train. I wanted to talk to him. I wanted his mouth to open and speak. I wanted him to look at me with his eyes.

"You're not the first person I've told that story to. This is very odd, actually. I once met a man in Palermo who was said to have fought a duel. It is a difficult story to believe. It is difficult to believe I met a man who claimed to have fought a duel, and it is difficult to believe that a man who said he had fought a duel had actually fought a duel. Everything about the duel was rumor from others—but it established his reputation, fable or not. But I wanted to hear the story firsthand, and there he was. So I said I knew a story of a man killed by a train. I offered to swap stories. He said nothing, but it seemed a silent agreement. So I told him the story, just as I have told you. When I had finished, he stood up from his chair, said, 'You have told me nothing,' and left the room. Of course I had told him nothing. I had been waiting for him to tell me."

"But you have to listen to people and make judgments about people all the time. So what did you conclude? Was he balls or bluster?"

"Greta, all I ever got out of the man was body language. And that was in reaction to his listening to *me*."

We do not get drunk. We never do. Neither of us overeat or overindulge in much of anything. We are not particularly demonstrative people.

We don't talk much about my book. It is a draining topic I've labored at for three years now. In that it's philosophy and not tied immediately to my profession, I have wondered whether I should employ a pseudonym when—and if—it is published. I do not believe in God; I believe in life; I believe it is my mission in life to make others believe in life rather than God.

At 6:30 p.m. I spend an hour on a stationary bike in the exercise room. It is a well-used room, with three or four bikes, a half-dozen treadmills, a rowing machine, and a weight machine. I set the one available bike at its highest resistance level and leave it there—no uphill-downhill course settings.

The ship has now turned west over the northern tip of Cape Breton Island and we are finally finding the storm.

The scene is wholly unexpected. The treadmills, the bikes, all the machines, face the sea, which we see through a wall of glass as though through a picture window. The evening sky has darkened and the ship's lights are on. Our vantage point is full ahead. A white mask of thickening snow burrows into us as if into headlights. We are sweating and the snow comes at us like Kamikazes ditching at the last second.

Against this setting I spend the hour reading Voltaire's *Candide*. If you long for depression to pull at your abnormal euphoria, *Candide* is for you.

My legs pump like a pedicab driver's, continuously, the task unending. My eyes momentarily release their grasp on *Candide*.

Where do we live, I ask myself. If we live within, entirely within, then "Prozac Nation" may be as good as we can do. But certainly that's foolish nonsense. If we live entirely within, we have the dilemma that was Ed Boschnägel as he neared the end. A head thinking, but unable to *do*. A tenure nearing an end, but nearing it at such a silky, infinitesimal pace, the magic of action—the privilege of volition—removed, did it really require a mind-reader to see what was needed? It required nothing magical to see what Greta saw, what she was forced to witness, day after meaningless day. Days of sordid rectitude, no reclamation of her singular sense of body-and-mind united, no resolute pace of life—hers could be the drifting emptiness of a tumbling snowflake—even a haiku has the luxury of brevity, but this was no haiku.

And my internal debate was always method, never whether. R_x pads are handy, of course, or you use whatever you have access to. It's accepted that at one stage or another, any ALS patient suffers depression, usually chronic. As for method, Prozac was impossible—all the newer anti-depressants protected against the one thing you feared most with a depressive patient—suicide by overdose. That still left the old reliable options, among them just about any barbiturates you cared to name. A single injection and no fear of autopsy. With ALS, death is expected.

Again I see the snow falling into the ship's lights. *Candide* returns to focus.

I have no working title for my philosophy book. *Candide* should provide good inspiration, but I spend too much time fixating on words that slide into my head from elsewhere. So many times my daydreams lead to this quite imaginary conversation with Greta. I see it as two lines of dialog in a play:

Greta: Did he ask you to?
Me: How could he, he couldn't speak. He couldn't even blink his eyes.

Truthfully, he could blink his eyes. I just never asked.

In my imagined disclosure, she is either grateful or forgiving, I don't know which. I shall hope for both, and never ask for fear of disappointment. She may know, or she may not. Even if she believes it, I cannot believe she will ever broach the subject. In a way, had I not done what I'd done she might not have come to write such good poetry. If she ever believed that, guilt would bring her poetry to a halt.

What she actually said—once the bouquets had withered or been strewn by cemetery winds—was something simpler, "Well, now, I suppose, we can get on with our lives." She did not blink, staring at me as if staring at my soul. Even from my patients, I have never heard or seen anything so enigmatic.

Long ago in the lost Vietnam year of my youth, at a firebase six miles from Cambodia, my enterprising buddies slipped half-a-dozen bargirls through the gates using an armored personnel carrier. But first the women all wanted showers. And there I was all alone taking my shower in a shower room built for ten when they came in. They were among the six friendliest girls I have ever met.

Descartes could probably have plotted a mathematical curve for distinguishing true, absolute friendship. Could a theoretical curve really portray something so important—predict our affiliations, our hates? The infinitesimal areas below such curves provide the rock hard basis for Newton's calculus, after all, and a point is a dimensionless abstraction upon which the soul of mathematics is based. So, is such a calculation possible ...? Will reading another thousand books help?

I live in such a mineshaft, but let's call it a cocoon. The mind has so many comforts and distractions for its ills. If only I could make everyone else see.

I devote myself entirely to the well-being of others. My occupation "occupies" me full-time. I'm married to no one. I've abused no one. I live a clean life. I've never used drugs. I've never divorced anyone. I've never had a child. I've never left anyone fatherless. I've never made a promise I didn't try with full diligence to keep. And once I saved someone's life by taking someone else's that was already gone.

At my office I keep a bust on my desk of a woman's head. It is smooth, well-proportioned, and very fine. If a patient asks who it is, I readily tell him, That is Anna's head. There are three likely responses. Some sit silently cogitating, assuming the bust is personal in nature and they will not ask. Some will say, Is this your wife? To those persons I merely smile. One person once asked me, Is it the head of Anna Karenina? To that person I replied, "Do you think this is the most beautiful head in the world?"

Descartes, they say, slept ten hours a day and never rose before noon. He spent all his time thinking. He never married. He did little else but think.

I am an earlier riser and an attendant for the sick-of-heart.

I used to run to think. Age has emptied me of my running days. Now I walk.

I am in good company.

Wallace Stevens walked and wrote poems in his head. Or he walked to a shop where he would admire fresh fruit, make a choice, and eat.

In Königsberg, Immanuel Kant used to walk a tree-lined lane that came to be known as The Philosopher's Walk. His neighbors could set their time by him: when he emerged from his house to walk, it was half-past three in the afternoon.

I've found I enjoy walking into a wind. The stronger the better, like an uphill project. Thinking is good labor.